THE ASTERISK WAR

16 · THE GOLDEN BOUGH · CONFLAGRATION

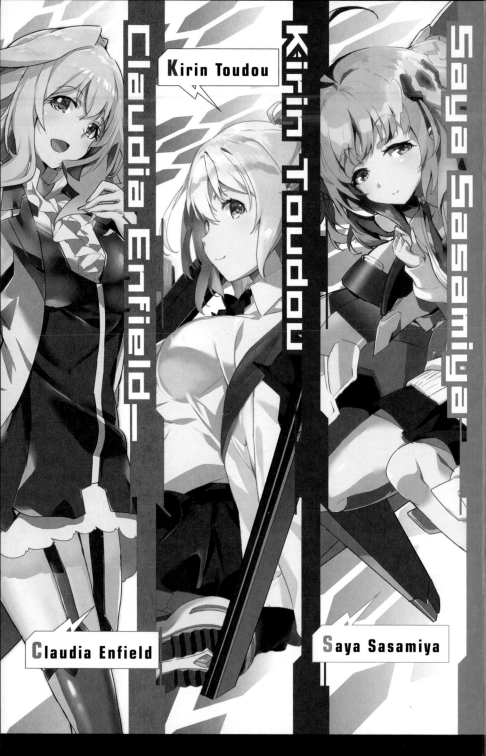

Claudia Enfield

Kirin Toudou

Saya Sasamiya

Kirin Toudou

Claudia Enfield

Saya Sasamiya

Julis-Alexia von Riessfeld

Julis-Alexia von Riessfeld

Ayato Amagiri

Ayato Amagiri

ser veresta

contents

THE ASTERISK WAR

16. THE GOLDEN BOUGH CONFLAGRATION

YUU MIYAZAKI
ILLUSTRATION: OKIURA

YEN ON

NEW YORK

THE ASTERISK WAR, Vol. 16
YUU MIYAZAKI

Translation by Haydn Trowell
Cover art by okiura

This book is a work of fiction. Names, characters, places, and incidents are the product of the author's imagination or are used fictitiously. Any resemblance to actual events, locales, or persons, living or dead, is coincidental.

© Yuu Miyazaki 2021
First published in Japan in 2021 by KADOKAWA CORPORATION.
English translation rights reserved by Yen Press, LLC under the license from KADOKAWA CORPORATION, Tokyo, through TUTTLE-MORI AGENCY, INC. Tokyo.

English translation © 2022 by Yen Press, LLC

Yen On
150 West 30th Street, 19th Floor
New York, NY 10001

Visit us at yenpress.com
facebook.com/yenpress
twitter.com/yenpress
yenpress.tumblr.com
instagram.com/yenpress

First Yen On Edition: November 2022
Edited by Thalia Sutton & Yen On Editorial: Emma McClain
Designed by Yen Press Design: Andy Swist

Yen On is an imprint of Yen Press, LLC.
The Yen On name and logo are trademarks of Yen Press, LLC.

The publisher is not responsible for websites (or their content) that are not owned by the publisher.

Library of Congress Cataloging-in-Publication Data
Names: Miyazaki, Yuu, author. | Tanaka, Melissa, translator. |
Trowell, Haydn, translator.
Title: The asterisk war / Yuu Miyazaki ; translation by Melissa Tanaka.
Other titles: Gakusen toshi asterisk. English
Description: First Yen On edition. | New York, NY : Yen On, 2016– |
v. 6–8 translation by Haydn Trowell | Audience: Ages 13 & up.
Identifiers: LCCN 2016023755 | ISBN 9780316315272 (v. 1 : paperback) |
ISBN 9780316398589 (v. 2 : paperback) | ISBN 9780316398602 (v. 3 : paperback) |
ISBN 9780316398626 (v. 4 : paperback) | ISBN 9780316398657 (v. 5 : paperback) |
ISBN 9780316398671 (v. 6 : paperback) | ISBN 9780316398695 (v. 7 : paperback) |
ISBN 9780316398718 (v. 8 : paperback) | ISBN 9781975302801 (v. 9 : paperback) |
ISBN 9781975329358 (v. 10 : paperback) | ISBN 9781975303518 (v. 11 : paperback) |
ISBN 9781975304317 (v. 12 : paperback) | ISBN 9781975304331 (v. 13 : paperback) |
ISBN 9781975359454 (v. 14 : paperback) | ISBN 9781975316396 (v. 15 : paperback) |
ISBN 9781975348601 (v. 16 : paperback)
Subjects: CYAC: Science fiction. | BISAC: FICTION / Science Fiction / Adventure.
Classification: LCC PZ7.1.M635 As 2016 | DDC [Fic]—dc23
LC record available at https://lccn.loc.gov/2016023755

ISBNs: 978-1-9753-4860-1 (paperback)
978-1-9753-4861-8 (ebook)

10 9 8 7 6 5 4 3 2 1

LSC-C

Printed in the United States of America

CHAPTER 1
THE SEMIFINALS II

Once every few years, various top executives from each of the integrated enterprise foundations would come together for the Concordia, a summit in which they would collectively make long-term adjustments to their corporate road maps. In so doing, they coordinated the interests under their control and determined the future of the world. This time, it was being held on a luxury cruise ship sailing the North Kanto Mass-Impact Crater Lake, not far from the city of Asterisk.

While their ostensible goal was to coordinate their activities, each of the IEFs was, in actuality, in direct competition with the others.

The organizations might join hands for one project or another, but there could be no mistaking that, as a general rule, each aimed to expand its own economic sphere of influence by ultimately eliminating the others.

For that reason, only *matters of catastrophic importance* were to be discussed at the Concordia. War, for instance—one of many political tools with the potential to bring a reasonable return on investment but that could also prove a considerable liability should events get out of hand and exceed a certain threshold.

Fortunately, the world hadn't seen a war on a global scale since the Invertia, though there had been several close calls. The armed conflict over Vertice Meteorites that had led to the demise of the former foundation Severclara was probably the most notable of these.

Since then, the integrated enterprise foundations had endeavored to avoid armed conflict as much as possible, each of them placing renewed emphasis on the importance of maintaining the balance of power. It was for this reason that the Concordia was held at regular intervals. In other words, the IEFs were, on a fundamental level, highly contradictory entities—they continuously sought out opportunities to destroy their competitors, but at the same time, they constantly feared any upset to the equilibrium that existed between them.

The only way this contradiction could be resolved was if one of the foundations wound up occupying a clear minority position. In the current setup, that meant if one of them was to go up against the other five, its only remaining option would be to go to war as the others sought to carve it up. Precisely to avoid such a situation, each of the organizations had entered into an intricate network of connecting interests.

Nonetheless, low-level skirmishes still tended to erupt every now and then throughout the world. Though rare, there were occasions when military units under the direct control of the foundations faced off against one another in violent confrontation without authorization from their upper echelons. Moreover, there were always countless cases of terrorist attacks against the foundations themselves.

As such, holding the Concordia at the same time as the Festa, and in such close proximity, made security preparations no small matter. And in a major tourist city, where untold numbers of visitors mingled every day and with so many Stregas and Dantes out and about, there could be no such thing as absolute assurances. Unexpected situations were all but guaranteed.

After much deliberation, it was decided to construct a cruise ship from the ground up to ensure adequate safety and confidentiality for the Concordia. Once the summit was over, the vessel would be converted into a sightseeing pleasure ship for the wealthy.

Well, at least things look like they're going to end without incident...

Breathing a sigh of relief, a member of Galaxy's security contingent stood close to the wall, quietly and unobtrusively watching the strangely tense exchange taking place in front of him.

The thirty people seated around the conference table were each top executives at one or another of the foundations. Despite their diverse ages, sexes, and ethnicities, they all seemed to be clones of each other—probably a result of the high-level psychological conditioning programs to which they had all been subjected.

Finally, this lengthy Concordia was reaching its end. The only event remaining on the schedule was to watch the championship match of the Festa the following day. So far, the only time the executives and their entourages had left the cruise ship was to inspect the tournament headquarters a few days prior.

When they had come to watch the Lindvolus last time, it had been from the special viewing lounges adjacent to the tournament headquarters, and no executives had been required to set foot in the venues themselves. But even that had been enough to make the members of their security details break out into a cold sweat.

Even now, behind the representatives of each organization, stood several security personnel ready to move at a moment's notice in response to any unforeseen developments. Naturally, in addition to the executives' own security details, there was an army of other security officers working twenty-four hours a day to ensure that the ship was fully protected, half of which had been assigned from Asterisk's city guard, Stjarnagarm.

It wasn't just during the Concordia that distribution of security personnel proved a major challenge. The same issues arose at most gatherings attended by executives from multiple foundations, though given their mutual distrust of one another, this wasn't particularly surprising. There wasn't a single corridor or doorway on this vessel that hadn't been the subject of some dispute, of a pitched debate as to precisely which security officers should man it.

In that respect, it was fortunate that Stjarnagarm, being independent of the six integrated enterprise foundations, could be called on this time around. It was a shame that this meant thinning the numbers of an already short-staffed police force (there could be no denying that this would further undermine Asterisk's own internal security), but the members of the city guard, handpicked by Commander Helga Lindwall herself, were excellent and dependable. Many of them had been leading students in Asterisk's Named Cult; they couldn't be bribed or bought off, and they had an unshakable sense of mission and duty. After all, if they had been concerned about money or status, they would have long since been scouted by one of the foundations—as he himself had been.

Yes, the man surveying the room was himself a former student of Asterisk, and he too had spent his youth participating in the Festa. At one point, he had even been a Page One. After graduating, he had been scouted by Galaxy and chosen the security division over its military affairs division.

Objectively speaking, the man had been a superb student in his own right, but not quite the best. The IEFs would no doubt continue to scout those who ranked higher than him—in other words, those who had stood at the very top of the rankings—to serve in their elite military divisions. But whether or not they signed up, this trend made it clear that the foundations favored offense over defense as a matter of principle.

In order to ensure the use of force could be adequately applied when necessary, the best talent (in terms of individual combat abilities) belonged not in the security division but in military affairs. The protection of VIPs was inevitably a secondary concern.

Why? To put it bluntly, for the IEFs, even top executives were no more than interchangeable parts. Of course, those parts weren't easy to come by, and it was true they served a necessary function for their organization.

However, if, for instance, everyone in this room was killed in a terrorist attack or tragic accident, the injury, though great, wouldn't be irreversible. The same would be the case even if those top executives not present were all lost at the same time, though that, of course, was unlikely. Yes, the damage would be immense and plans would be set back to a certain extent, but the foundations themselves would go on. The loss wouldn't be so grave as to change the trajectory of the world as a whole.

For this reason, the foundations would invest a reasonable amount of human and financial resources to stave off such a loss but would go no further. The construction of this luxury cruise ship and the tight security surrounding it were all part of that delicate cost-benefit analysis.

The integrated enterprise foundations were like ravenous monsters. They would sooner sharpen their fangs to rend their prey than defend themselves—all to become even bigger, even stronger, until, when the time came, their innate contradictions would resurface, and they would set about tearing one another apart again.

Well, that's a little above the pay grade of a mere security officer...

The man chuckled to himself as he checked the status throughout the ship using the small air-window at his hand. He knew that his job was ultimately meaningless, but it was still his job. He had to do it. Besides, weren't most forms of work in this world ultimately pointless?

It was true. At this point, no matter what you did, there was very little on this planet you could change.

The rule of the foundations was absolute, and people had come to accept that. After all, they had entrenched their positions through amending government policy over the decades.

Of course, there would always be a certain number of people who refused to accept the status quo, but they were only a small minority. They weren't capable of calling others to action. Even if, somehow, they were to kill everyone gathered here, it might have some minor impact, but nothing more. It wouldn't be enough to rouse people's hearts and minds. It wouldn't open so much as a single crack in the system.

The world would *never* change.

Or would it?

*

"*Yeeeaaahhh! It's time for the last match of the Lindvolus semifinals! Our contestants are about to step into the arena! For better or for worse, there are only two matches left! Who will it be?! Who will face off against Julis-Alexia von Riessfeld in the championship?! There she is—our strongest, invincible, undefeated defending champion is stepping out from the West Gate! Having annihilated Sigrdrífa in the quarterfinals, her rival Sylvia Lyyneheym, here she is, Erenshkigal herself, Orphelia Landlufen!*"

Saya stared at Orphelia's figure from where she stood, just behind the doorway of the East Gate. Her opponent's pure-white hair swayed as she advanced onto the bridge that led down to the arena, her grand entrance accompanied by a bombardment of deafening cheers and dazzling lights.

Frankly, Saya had never expected to make it this far. To be perfectly honest, fate had lent her a helping hand. If even one small detail had been different—be it the tournament brackets or the events of her matches thus far—it would have been someone else standing here now.

Nonetheless, it was she who had made it to this point.

Her original goal—settling her score with Rimcy—might have been rendered impossible, but she had at least been able to fulfil her duty by defeating Lenaty, and she was content with that victory. However, the injuries to her arms were worse than she had imagined, and she couldn't handle her Luxes as well as she would have liked. It would be impossible for her to land a precise attack in her current state. Even in perfect condition, defeating Orphelia was a long shot—but as she was now, she could hardly put up a fight. Which was why she had resolved to withdraw.

And yet...not too long ago, a thought had suddenly occurred to her:

Whether through skill or blind luck, she *had* survived the tournament thus far, so perhaps there was some meaning to her success.

The more she thought about it, the stronger that tiny voice in the back of her mind urged her to keep trying.

Of course, it would be an utterly meaningless endeavor. It was dangerous, it offered no clear benefit, and the outcome was all but guaranteed. Anyone else would dismiss the idea as folly.

And yet...

"...I guess there's no harm in giving it a go," she murmured under her breath as she stepped through the East Gate to the adjoining bridge.

"*Making her way through the East Gate is Saya Sasamiya of Seidoukan Academy, having just defeated Allekant Académie's latest autonomous puppet in the quarterfinals with a humongous, absolutely insane Lux that left the whole world stupefied! As I'm sure our viewers know, Sasamiya was a member of Team Enfield, the winners of last year's Gryps, so if she wins here, she'll be only the second person in history to reach the championship match in both tournaments!*"

"*I'll be honest with you, the odds of that are pretty unlikely.*" The voice of the announcer, Mico Yanase, was quickly cut off by that of the commentator, Zaharoula. "*From what I could see during her quarterfinal match, Saya Sasamiya sustained considerable damage. Frankly, I'd be surprised if she can even compete.*"

"*You think she won't be up to the challenge, even with that massive new Lux of hers?*"

"*That thing takes a good while to charge. I doubt Orphelia Landlufen will give her enough time.*"

Yeah, yeah, Saya thought. *You think I don't know all that?*

Her type 42 super-large caliber particle cannon, Neunfairdelph, was the strongest weapon she had prepared for the Festa. She was confident its raw power alone was potent enough to defeat Orphelia, but she understood full well there was no way she would be able to buy enough time—nine hundred and ninety-nine seconds—to activate it.

As she leaped from the bridge to the stage below, Orphelia's twin red eyes fixed on her with a look of resignation. Her expression was neither contemptuous nor condescending, betraying only a hint of sadness. She seemed utterly disinterested in her opponent.

No doubt that was true.

As far as Saya could tell from the video recordings of Orphelia's prior matches, the only foes who had been able to prompt any kind of emotional response from her were those with whom she had a history—namely Sylvia and Hilda Jane Rowlands. Right now, Saya was just one more opponent, the next in line to be slaughtered.

But that won't do...

With a soft smile, she tapped the microphone attached to her collar.

Orphelia, noticing the gesture, shut hers off, too. "What?" she asked with indifference.

Saya was grateful to be able to jump straight to the point. "There's just one thing I want to get off my chest."

"Go ahead."

"I didn't come here today to fight."

Orphelia's brow rose quizzically. "Oh? What do you mean?"

"I came here to talk to you."

The young woman across from her slowly shook her head. "I see. Unfortunately, I have nothing to say."

Saya had expected this response. After all, the two of them had never met, and she doubted that Orphelia knew much about her.

Nonetheless...

"I think you do. Because I'm here as a friend of Julis-Alexia von Riessfeld."

"…" Orphelia remained devoid of expression.

Yet Saya couldn't miss the fact that *something* had flashed for the briefest of moments behind her resignation and grief.

"You're a friend of hers, too. So let's talk, right here, right now."

This time, Orphelia's eyebrow twitched visibly. "No. That's in the past. All of it. It has nothing to do with me anymore. More importantly, it has nothing to do with you."

Those twin red eyes remained fixed on Saya.

The malicious intent emanating from her body was extraordinary. Just standing before her, the feeling of intimidation was enough to extinguish Saya's heart.

But now, it seemed Orphelia had finally acknowledged her as her own person.

First steps, right?

Sucking in her breath, she caught Orphelia's gaze and fixed her with a sharp glare. "Nothing to do with me? You can't mean that…!"

She let a hint of anger creep into her voice as she continued, "I don't know the details. Julis doesn't tell us anything. But I'm sure she's silent out of consideration for us. Because she…she cherishes me, and Kirin, and Claudia, and Haru, and Ayato. And despite that, she chose you."

She thrust her finger in Orphelia's face. "And yet you say it's all in the past, that it has nothing to do with you anymore… How can I stand by and ignore that?!"

"…What else *can* you do?" Orphelia whispered, activating the Gravisheath and holding it loosely before her.

The tension had risen to a fever pitch, the air itself all but sparking with excitement.

"I'll crush you! …At least, that's what I'd like to say, but I know it's beyond me now." Saya heaved a sigh, letting her shoulders droop. "So like I said, I just want to talk. About what *you're* going to do. I don't know why Julis is so hell-bent on stopping you. If I did, I might be able to understand. Because that's how you come to a mutual understanding. By talking."

Seemingly caught off guard, Orphelia shook her head before slowly lowering the Gravisheath. "You really came all this way just to talk?"

"That's what I've been saying from the start."

"You didn't think I'd just defeat you without answering your questions?"

"Well, I'm ready for that possibility, too."

In fact, Saya knew the odds were quite high she would do just that.

Nine out of ten, if someone asked her to wager on it. After all, what reason would Orphelia have to engage her in conversation?

And yet…

Julis's feelings were strong enough to compel her to face off against Orphelia.

In that case, Orphelia should be able to accept just as much. Saya hoped that was the case, at least. It ought to be.

If not, it would be too tragic for Julis.

"Yes… I see you're determined."

Orphelia's eyes narrowed. "But are you prepared to forfeit your life?"

"—!"

Every hair on Saya's body stood on end.

That was no idle threat—Orphelia was being completely serious.

In fact, Orphelia had stopped Sylvia's heart during their quarter-final match. *She* might have been successfully revived immediately afterward, but it wasn't guaranteed that Saya would be so lucky.

"Of course I don't want to die… But, well, if that's what it takes."

Her answer didn't mean she had no problem with dying—only that she suspected, hoped, that her opponent wouldn't use any techniques that would actually threaten her life.

The Stella Carta expressly prohibited acts of intentional cruelty, as well as those intended to kill. Of course, it could be difficult to distinguish between a strike meant from the very beginning to end another's life and one that did so inadvertently, so the rule wasn't strictly enforced.

But even so, there *had* just been the incident with Sylvia. Orphelia had already been reprimanded for engaging in overly dangerous conduct, and even if there hadn't been any real penalty, should it happen a second time... Maybe. Then again, maybe not.

"...Okay. I'll keep you company for a little while, then. Your fate is fragile, but you seem to be riding a strange turn of events."

"Huh...?"

With those words, Orphelia spun around and returned to her starting position.

It was time, Saya realized, for the match to get underway.

"I'll answer your questions. So long as you're still standing."

"...Good."

In other words, if she wanted to get as much information out of Orphelia as possible, she would have to keep fending off her attacks.

"Lindvolus Semifinals, Match 2—begin!"

No sooner had the starting signal sounded than Saya deployed her vernier unit around her legs and hips.

The Luxes destroyed in the match against Lenaty remained severely damaged, and there was no way she could repair them all overnight, if at all. This vernier unit was just a spare. It had taken a lot of work to configure, but without it, she couldn't compete.

"Tch!"

She immediately set about evading several plumes of miasma that Orphelia sent arcing her way, gliding backward across the stage. The tendrils continued to pursue her, forcing her to throw out a small object that she kept close to her chest.

At that moment, a fierce blast of wind exploded around her, accompanied by a dazzling flash and a tremendous roar.

"Whoa! Was that an explosion?!"

"Heh... Now that's *unusual*. A *Mana Grenade*. Probably customized, judging by its power just now."

Saya's Mana Grenades, as the name suggested, were explosive

weapons powered by manadite crystals. Unlike normal Luxes, the mana embedded in each could only be used once, so they weren't exactly cheap to manufacture. And since they required separate triggers, the advantage of typical grenades—their compact size— wasn't applicable. As a result, they weren't often seen in Asterisk.

However, they did have unique advantages, such as allowing her to control the direction of the blast and easily adjust the power and timing of each detonation. It would have been impossible to use a regular grenade at close range, as she had just now, without getting caught in the explosion herself.

Most of all, their use put very little strain on her arms. In her current state, unable to aim with precision or withstand the recoil of her large-caliber Luxes, this was the perfect weapon. And as Zaharoula had pointed out, she and her father Souichi had set about boosting the power of the grenades.

And, of course, they're good for dealing with Erenshkigal's miasma.

Since Orphelia's toxic miasma was a gas, it couldn't be dealt with using ordinary armaments. Just as a blade couldn't slice through a poisonous cloud, neither could a regular Lux—that would take the abilities of a Strega or Dante. Saya might have been able to blow the gas away with a well-timed burst of her high-powered Luxes, but even then, she would be constantly one step behind her opponent, who could quickly overwhelm her. In that respect, these Mana Grenades were particularly useful at dispersing Orphelia's toxins.

There was only one problem—her limited supply. This time, Saya hadn't brought any Luxes with her except for her Helnekraum, which had survived the previous match intact. Naturally, she lacked her S-Module, too. Instead, she had prepared as many Mana Grenades as she could carry, but even after attaching them to the inside of her uniform and to the holders around her waist, she could only equip sixteen in total. She didn't need to worry about setting them off, but carrying any more at once would inevitably hinder her movements.

In other words, she only had fifteen left.

"…"

Orphelia remained unfazed, summoning up fresh plumes of miasma, which rose from beneath her feet.

Well, Saya had expected as much. Orphelia's defensive power, fueled by her all but limitless reserves of prana, was extraordinary. Even if Saya did manage to catch her at close range in an explosion, how much damage would it really inflict?

But, of course, her goal here wasn't victory.

"All right then, first question: What are you guys—the Golden Bough Alliance—trying to achieve? What's your goal?"

She decided to start with the most pressing concern.

Given all the circumstantial evidence, there could be no doubt that Orphelia was a member of the Golden Bough Alliance.

Despite all the frantic investigations that Saya herself—that Kirin, Ayato, Sylvia, Claudia, Captain Helga and Haruka over at Stjarnagarm, Eishirou in Seidoukan Academy's own intelligence branch, and Claudia's mother Isabella, a top executive at Galaxy—had seen to, they still hadn't been able to figure out what the Golden Bough Alliance was truly up to.

If she could secure an answer to this question alone, getting here would have been worth it.

"Who knows? I certainly don't. I'm not interested in their plans," Orphelia replied, readying the Gravisheath.

The next moment, a number of jet-black gravitational spheres came hurtling toward Saya. Orphelia had used the same projectiles in her match against Sylvia, and now she had sent more than a hundred flying across the field, forcing Saya to cast out two more of her Mana Grenades as she fell back—but not before twin tendrils of miasma slipped through her defensive counter.

"Tch!"

Left with no other choice, she tossed one more to defend herself. Now her stock was down to twelve.

But that couldn't be her priority right now.

Orphelia didn't seem to be lying. If she wasn't willing to speak honestly, she wouldn't have bothered to engage in dialogue at all.

In that case, Saya needed to think of a better question.

"...What are *you* to the Golden Bough Alliance?" she asked again, weaving through the pursuing miasma.

"I'm...an essential part of their plan, you might say."

Bingo.

Saya wasted no time before coming out with a follow-up: "Then what *is* your role in their plans?"

Orphelia came to a sudden halt. "...I can answer you, but if I do, there will be no turning back. Are you ready?"

"I was born ready."

"You realize Julis left your group to spare you from this, don't you?"

"What a load of crap. I don't know what burden she's carrying, but we're strong enough to shoulder it together."

No sooner had Saya finished speaking than Orphelia's eyes flashed with something other than resignation and grief—but as for whether that expression's true nature was anger, jealousy, pity, or even envy, Saya couldn't tell.

"...I see. Yes, I did say you were determined. In that case, I'll tell you."

"...!"

At that moment, Orphelia closed the distance between them in a split second.

Her current foe wasn't the type to engage in melee combat, so her sudden movement caught Saya off guard—but she quickly activated her vernier and beat a hasty retreat, the tip of the Gravisheath passing directly before her eyes and slicing clean through her fringe.

And with that lunge, she heard Orphelia murmur:

"To kill you. All of you."

*

Kirin stopped in her tracks to the sound of loud cheers erupting around her.

She was in the Rotlicht in Asterisk's redevelopment area.

The sun was still out, which meant that a good many shops had yet to open their doors. The crowds weren't quite as large as would be expected at night, but there was still a lively commotion in front of a large screen set up at the street corner. A full half of the crowd were clearly outsiders—in other words, tourists—and the other half probably worked in the nightclubs that could be found throughout the Rotlicht, or else belonged to the organized crime groups that made it their stronghold.

The screen, of course, was showing the semifinal match between Saya and Orphelia.

Kirin glanced up to catch a glimpse of Saya's desperate struggle... then immediately shook her head and scurried away.

She wanted to support her, she really did—but right now, she had her own mission to complete.

And above all, Saya herself had forbidden her from interfering.

"...I don't need support. I'm not planning to win anyway. I want you all on the tail of the Golden Bough Alliance."

That was what she had said, and Kirin had been unable to voice any objections.

Still, she wanted to do everything in her power to help.

Just as Ayato considered Julis his cherished tag team partner, so too did Kirin consider Saya hers.

Even if Saya didn't intend to win this fight, there was no telling what might happen to her in a contest against Orphelia Landlufen. It would quite literally be a battle for survival.

Saya knew that, of course, but still she had decided to meet her opponent in the arena. Not for herself, but for Julis. For her friends.

"If Orphelia is part of the Golden Bough Alliance, we might be able to get some information out of her. But even if we can't, we might still be able to help Julis some other way. Of course, I'll throw in the towel if things look bad, so don't worry."

With those words, Saya had adopted her usual confident pose, making a victory sign with her fingers.

As that image flashed again before her eyes, Kirin warmed with pride.

If she's willing to go that far, I'll need to do my best, too...!

Her mission was to locate Madiath Mesa, whose whereabouts were presently unknown.

Of course, without any clues to go off, that wasn't exactly an easy task.

If you wanted to lie low in Asterisk, the easiest place to do so was the redevelopment area, the Rotlicht in particular. The second best option would probably be the city's underground block.

Both were presently the subject of extensive investigation by Stjarnagarm, but with the city guard's shortage of manpower, they couldn't search everywhere.

In any case, Kirin needed intel, which was why she was about to make contact with a certain mafia boss at Claudia's request. Although not as extensive as the intelligence agencies run by the various schools, the information networks of Asterisk's organized crime groups weren't to be underestimated. Moreover, since this particular group was staunchly opposed to Le Wolfe, it was less likely to be under Dirk's sway.

To be honest, Kirin *was* a little worried about dealing with the mafia, but with Eishirou's help and Claudia's guidance (probably based on information from one of their rival organizations), she had brought a small present to get started on the right foot. She would manage, somehow. By this point, Ayato would probably be looking into another such group, in order to boost their chances of success.

I—I am scared, but...I can do this!

She was always scared, always giving in to her own cowardice— but now, forcing herself to regain her composure, she glanced over her shoulder.

The screen was showing a close-up of Saya's face, awash with grim determination as she fought to survive Orphelia's onslaught.

*

"To kill you. All of you."

Saya felt her whole body break out in a cold sweat. Her heart was racing.

Not because she had only narrowly escaped being decapitated by the Gravisheath—but because Orphelia's voice rang with the terrifying tone of truth.

"Kill? All of us? What do you mean…?"

She just couldn't understand.

"Exactly what I said. My role is to kill everyone in this place…no, this whole *city*."

Saya was at a loss for words. "That's…"

"Impossible? No, I can do it. Surely you must be aware. The poison produced by my abilities can be adapted in effect and potency. Of course, all it would take is a single drop to end a person's life."

Her voice filled with self-assurance, Orphelia drew in the miasma roiling at her feet, playing with it as it coiled around her arms.

"You need to keep it at a certain concentration to control it like this, but without that control, it would spread all over this man-made island. There would be no containing it, then. I could destroy the entire protective field encasing this stage right now."

"…"

Saya shuddered but fought to regain her composure and think.

If—if Orphelia really did that, the number of casualties would be terrifyingly high. After all, this stadium alone currently housed more than a hundred thousand spectators. On top of that, Asterisk was one of the world's leading tourist destinations, and it was now the height of travel season. If you added to that all the people living in the city's residential districts and the students of the six schools, the number would be even higher.

"However, if I were to let my abilities burn out of control, my body would be unable to keep up. So I wouldn't be here to see the outcome for myself." Her tone matter-of-fact, Orphelia twisted the miasma circling around her into a giant arm. "*Kur nu Gia.*"

A single Mana Grenade wouldn't be enough to disperse a cloud of miasma that size.

Left with no other choice, Saya cast three of her explosives all at once, letting loose a storm-like blast that stopped the arm of toxins reaching out to her in its tracks. Nonetheless, she had failed to completely dissolve it, and the arm maintained its form. Clicking her tongue in dismay, she added another two Mana Grenades.

Now she was down to only seven.

"Are you willing to give up your own life? Even when you don't know their endgame...?!" Saya cried, pushing her vernier unit as hard as it would go. She fell back as several more miasma tendrils reached out to snare her.

"Didn't you hear me? They didn't refuse to tell me. I just wasn't interested in listening. Of course, I do remember how when Dirk Eberwein took charge of me, he went on about changing the world or something like that... Well, I'm sure you've heard that story before. My life means nothing to me anymore. Everything comes second to my fate," Orphelia stated plainly.

"You've got to be kidding! What kind of fate is that?!"

It was unimaginable, unforgivable, to take the lives of so many for such an incomprehensible reason.

With any other opponent, she might have lashed out in anger at these remarks—but right now, her priority had to be to get as much information as possible while she still could.

Calming her passions as she dodged the miasma tendrils, she ran left and right across the stage until finally she was cornered, forced to cast out another two Mana Grenades to survive Orphelia's unrelenting assault.

Five left now.

"Does Julis know all this?"

"Yes. I told her."

"Then…"

In that case, was Julis trying to solve this by herself?

But it seemed too urgent, too enormous, for her to keep secret merely out of concern for her childhood friend. She should have reported a threat of this magnitude to Stjarnagarm immediately, or even left it to the IEFs themselves to deal with. The security forces would have been able to take formal precautions, such as securing evidence—though the foundations, if left to themselves, would probably have tried to solve it by disposing of Orphelia, just as they had attempted to eliminate Claudia in the past.

However great Orphelia's value to them, surely Solnage, which backed Le Wolfe, wouldn't have hesitated to do just that. And if they did, then all six of the foundations would become Orphelia's enemy, and as powerful as she was, she was still just one person. She would only be able to resist so far.

"You're wondering why Julis hasn't acted yet, aren't you?" Orphelia asked, as though reading her mind.

Then with a swing of the Gravisheath, she summoned up a second barrage of gravitational spheres.

"The answer is simple: because the game has already begun."

"Huh…?"

Saya was forced to hurl two more Mana Grenades, reducing her stock to three.

"It certainly wouldn't be that hard to stop me, if the right organization took the appropriate steps. They could exert pressure, plan an assassination, or dispatch a squad of elite troops to eliminate me by force. But the situation has moved far beyond that point now."

"Far beyond that…?"

"They've been reaching out to collaborators for a very long time. You already know, I'm sure. The Lux with mental interference abilities, the one capable of brainwashing people? They already have Stjarnagarm and the foundations in the palm of their hand. Of course, those collaborators aren't always entirely compliant, and they're not always in the highest of positions. They might not be able to call off an operation once it gets underway... But even so, they serve as eyes and ears."

Lowering her hand, Orphelia called off her attack for a moment. "If they ever suspected that someone had caught on to me or to the Golden Bough Alliance, the plan was supposed to be put in motion. Ideally, it was to take place after the Lindvolus's championship match, but that isn't a strict requirement. They could have initiated it at any time—today, tomorrow, yesterday, a week ago, even last year if they had felt like it. All they need to do is give me the order."

Saya's breath caught in her throat.

Did that mean the Golden Bough Alliance had already won?

In other words, if she was to tell anyone about Orphelia's purpose, she would in effect trigger a large-scale terrorist attack?

No wonder Julis had decided not to share that information and instead tried to find a solution by herself. She hadn't had any other choice.

Strictly speaking, she could have fled to save her own life at the expense of everyone else's, but she would have never chosen that path.

Has Julis been struggling with this secret the whole time?

Saya herself was almost crushed by the weight of what she had just learned. No, no one should be forced to protect a secret that could spell the end of more than a million lives.

"...!"

At that moment, an unprecedented volley of miasma tendrils shot toward her.

She immediately threw two of her remaining Mana Grenades but was unable to block all of the attack and was forced at the last minute to release her final explosive. Her stock was now empty, zero.

In any event, she needed to fall back...

With that thought occupying her brain, she was just about to increase the output of her vernier unit when she fell crashing to the ground.

"Gah...?!"

Is this the Gravisheath's...?!

Glancing up, she saw that the Orga Lux was radiating an eerie, pale glow.

While the weapon's basic ability increased the gravitational force exerted on a designated target area, since those coordinates needed to be precisely defined, it was supposed to be ineffective on an opponent as fast-moving as she was now.

And yet, as Saya tried desperately to claw out of the weapon's range, Orphelia spoke. "It's useless," she said. "The Gravisheath is affecting everything on this stage except the area immediately surrounding me."

"..."

The Orga Lux's former user, Irene Urzaiz, had only been able to pull off that trick by overloading the weapon, but it seemed Orphelia could now do so with ease.

Nonetheless, while Orphelia herself remained cool and soft-spoken, a low, jarring, grating sound emerged from the Gravisheath, like a voice replete with suffering and enmity.

"Are you satisfied? Now you share Julis's secret." Orphelia spoke darkly, staring down at her. "But don't worry. You won't have to suffer anymore."

Tendrils of her miasma unfurled, rising one by one around her feet, like arms rearing up from hell.

"Given your prana...this should be about enough poison, I suppose? When you wake up, it will be too late. Either that, or you will never wake again. Perhaps that too is your destiny."

Hearing those words, Saya realized something:

The poison that had affected Ayato during his fight with Orphelia in Lieseltania had affected his prana, forcing it to deplete itself. The greater one's innate reserves, the stronger the effect would be.

In that case, this was no time to hesitate.

"Ngh...!"

Compelling her aching limbs to move, she dragged the activation body of her Lux from its holder.

A huge gun barrel manifested before her, the weapon plunging hard into the ground. Saya, however, paid that no mind, using the LOBOS transition method to pour all her energy into its core—right up to the point that it risked exploding.

"Type thirty-eight Lux grenade launcher, Helnekraum—*Full Blast!*"

The same moment Saya pulled the trigger, Orphelia's miasma arms raced toward her all at once.

Even though it had been fired without proper aiming, with a deafening roar, the burst of light that erupted from the gun struck Orphelia head-on.

The ensuing blast and shock wave were even more powerful than that of Saya's Mana Grenades.

Nonetheless, when the dust cleared, Orphelia was standing there nonplussed, her hand outstretched.

Did she stop all that with just her left hand…?

And using nothing more than her prana…?

Her defenses, it seemed, were just as robust as Lenaty's armored plating.

Her consciousness quickly fading, Saya glared back at the pair of crimson eyes watching her from above.

What she saw there was unmistakably something other than grief and resignation.

*

"*And there we have it, the second semifinal match has been decided! As expected, the winner is none other than Orphelia Landlufen! That said, I don't think it went down exactly as we had all been anticipating, so why don't you let our viewers hear your thoughts, Zaharoula?*"

"*Yes, well, it looked to me like Saya Sasamiya never intended to aim for victory. First of all—*"

In the dimly lit corridor leading up to the prep room, Julis, who had been watching the match alone with her back to the wall, let out a small sigh and closed the air-window.

She had known how it would end from the very beginning.

And yet, Saya had insisted on challenging Orphelia, saying she wanted to try a new approach.

Julis hadn't been able to tell whether she had succeeded, but judging from Orphelia's behavior, somehow different from her usual self, Saya may indeed have accomplished her goals to some extent.

"That girl does try the strangest things, wouldn't you say?" a child-like figure said from the doorway, cackling. It was Xinglou Fan.

"…So you came."

"Of course. Ah, yours was a brilliant spectacle. To think you over-whelmed the Murakumo. It must have hurt to be forced to show your trump card early, no?"

"I didn't have any other choice. I wouldn't have been able to beat him without resorting to my *Queen of the Night* technique… But hold on, what do you mean exactly? Saya *tries the strangest things…*? Do you know what she was doing down there?"

Xinglou nodded solemnly. "I read her lips. It seems that fight was but a pretense to engage her foe in dialogue."

"To talk with her…? In the middle of a match? Against *Orphelia*?"

"Oh-ho-ho! A bold move indeed," Xinglou chuckled. "The mark of a true friend, no?"

Julis recognized at once just how reckless that course of action had been.

Orphelia rarely wasted her time during a match. Whether she was facing off against a strong opponent or a weak one, she would do everything within her power to overwhelm them at the first opportunity.

The notion of talking to her, of engaging her in dialogue, would normally be unthinkable.

But the way she looked to have been conversing with Saya…

"Do you know what they said?"

"Well, I wouldn't go that far. It isn't quite so easy, with them both flying all over the stage nonstop. That stripling in particular likes to hide behind her explosions... But it was something about that crazy plot hatched up by Orphelia's associates."

"...!" Julis found herself staring back at Xinglou in shock.

"Don't tell me you already know everything?"

Julis was certainly in Xinglou's debt, but her response here, if she wasn't careful, could end up ruining their relationship.

"Oh? You have a strong spirit, I see. You're getting good at this, aren't you?" Xinglou didn't seem perturbed in the slightest by Julis's gaze, fixing her with a satisfied grin. "Oh, don't glare. Yes, I too know of them. They even invited me to join. But I've never given them that satisfaction. All I know of their plan...is that they're trying to cause a second Invertia."

Was this the same plan that Haruka had previously undermined?

"I'm afraid I don't know their current agenda, but if it's anything like it was last time, I'm quite certain it's nothing good."

"..."

Julis stared hard into Xinglou's eyes, her tension gradually easing. She could discern no lie behind those words.

"All right. I'll believe you... But I do have another question."

"Oh? What now?"

"Couldn't *you* bring an end to their plans?"

That task was difficult enough for Julis even with the help of Ayato, Stjarnagarm, and the foundations, but surely the Ban'yuu Tenra ought to have the strength and ability?

"Perhaps. It certainly wouldn't be easy. But then again, it wouldn't be impossible, either."

"In that case—"

"But I'm afraid I can't." Xinglou cut her off. "I am unbound by the laws of this world. Should I so wish, none would be able to stop me—no human laws, no IEF. Only the rules that I have set for myself."

"You mean…you've set the rules that govern your existence by yourself?"

"Yes." Xinglou nodded. Her words were jarring considering she looked like an uninhibited, free-spirited girl. "One of those rules is to refrain from interfering with major affairs. To play no role in affecting the future of the world or the present age. And that is precisely what *they* seek to do. The future should always be decided by those who belong in the present. People like me, no longer fully of this world, shouldn't get involved."

The childish aspect to Xinglou's countenance vanished, and her face took on an almost supernatural cast.

"I enjoy a good contest of skill, but I don't seek conflict. I'm tired of war. If I break this prohibition, that is surely where my actions will lead. I have no desire to be a part of it."

"But even if you don't do anything, it will still happen! Conflict! War!"

"Indeed. The outcome is not the issue. There will always be a cause. That is something for you, those who properly live in this age, to bear."

"I thought you said you love Asterisk? Even if it meant the whole city would be destroyed, you'd still stand by and do nothing?"

"Indeed. Yes, I like it here. But that is no reason for me to break the rules that govern my actions. I respect myself too much. I will not violate them." Xinglou's answer was unwavering.

"I get it. One last question, then." Julis exhaled deeply, then looked straight into her counterpart's eyes. "Even if it costs the lives of your students, you still won't act?"

At that moment, the expression that rose to Xinglou's face was, surprisingly, a smile.

It wasn't her usual innocent look, not one of exuberance as when she was relishing a fight, but a glimmer cloaked in empty desolation— akin, in a way, to Orphelia's soft smile.

"…What do you know? I have lost so much, said farewell to so many. The people I loved, places to return to, times of peace… They are all but fleeting moments in time. My answer remains the same." Xinglou gazed back into Julis's eyes, giving her a quiet nod. "I will do nothing."

Behind her answer, Julis sensed a tremendous, absolute loneliness, and she was reminded once more that the small, childish figure before her existed beyond the usual human frame of reference. No matter how strong one was, no ordinary person would be able to withstand such desolation.

"All right. I think I get it. I haven't come this far to rely on others anyway," she said, turning her back on Xinglou.

It wasn't meant as a show of courage. The only thing she wanted was to free herself from any lingering regrets that might have come from paths not taken.

As she stepped forward to leave, a voice called out behind her: "Wait, Julis."

"What?"

As she glanced over her shoulder, Xinglou tossed her a gourd tied with red string.

"Take it—my apology for making you listen to my silly ramblings."

"What is it?"

"A Zhuojintang, a kind of sage elixir. Just something I give my students when the mood strikes me, nothing more."

Xinglou's face returned to her usual faint grin.

"It's capable of restoring depleted prana, at least to an extent. It's only intended to offer relief, but as the Chinese name suggests, it contains both water and metal properties as per the five phases. Your fire phase is often disordered, so if used at the right time, it may help you improve the circulation of your qi, which should in turn improve your prana recovery time."

"…I'll take it."

Even if it provided nothing more than peace of mind, Julis was grateful for the gesture.

"I'm looking forward to the championship match tomorrow. To a spectacle...and to your victory."

"..."

Julis offered no response, simply raising her left hand in a gesture of farewell as she turned to leave.

CHAPTER 2
POISON AND
CORRUPTION

It lasted only the briefest of moments.

In the world on *this side*, at least.

Orphelia, hooked to a machine at the mana collider test facility in Geneva, glimpsed a sudden vision and glanced frightfully toward Hilda Jane Rowlands.

Through a *hole* in her very consciousness, she established a *link* with another spirit.

When she came to, Orphelia found herself staring down at a huge, blue planet. She was now in space—or more precisely, in the outer atmosphere.

She had no physical sensation, and she couldn't see her own body. It was as if she'd been thrown out of it, and all that was left now was her consciousness.

She was so confused that it took her a moment to realize that the planet below her was Earth. But even if she had been clear of mind, no doubt she would have failed to recognize it at first. That was because its shape was different to the Earth she knew—the continents and oceans were similar, but certainly not the same.

Even so, at that moment, she understood on some vague level that she was staring down at *a* planet Earth.

All of a sudden, *something*, some huge entity, reached toward her consciousness.

As it made contact, her mind was shattered into pieces. The difference in scale between the two of them was simply too immense. It lacked substance, and its form—a pure mass of information—would have been unrecognizable to most humans. Yet that overwhelming force of power distorted the space around it through its very existence. If she had to give it a name, she would call it a god.

By all rights, that being ought to have diffused her consciousness out of existence, yet the divine force restored her mind before that could happen. Nonetheless, the process was imperfect—perhaps that task was too much even for a god to complete.

Why the entity put her back together, Orphelia didn't know.

The divine was too immense for any human to possibly understand.

It wasn't just language that proved insufficient—its manner of thought was simply too foreign as well.

Nonetheless, through this contact, Orphelia was finally able to comprehend the human world, albeit only in vague terms. In a way, the god made it possible for her to understand.

The world known as *the other side*.

A planetary system filled with *mana*.

A universe where *gods* existed.

It was a world so different to that on *this side*. There, each planet was inhabited by a single deity. Those gods possessed absolute authority within their spheres of influence and were literally omniscient and omnipotent. It was precisely because of that power that so many people were capable of living on distant planets, whereas on *this side*, only the Earth was inhabitable.

Those gods protected people, but at the same time, they were capable of taking life in huge numbers, either through natural disaster or more directly as divine retribution. The people on *this side*, Orphelia included, couldn't hope to comprehend such entities. Civilization had progressed through the use of meteoric engineering, and people were even capable of crossing the stars, but still they couldn't dream of communicating with the divine.

And so people on *the other side* possessed an unshakable faith in fate.

No matter how unreasonable, no matter how tragic, they had no choice but to accept the actions of the Absolute.

It was a horrifying, beautiful sense of resignation.

Fate...

An unknown emotion welled up in Orphelia's consciousness, imperfectly restored to a warped state.

And the next moment, her awareness returned to her *own side* of reality.

The next day, Orphelia was transferred to Frauenlob's research institute in Lieseltania.

From that moment on, her life was a living hell.

"Aaaaarrrrgggggghhhhh!"

Her screams tore her throat to shreds, blood foaming from her mouth. Her limbs, fixed to observation equipment, convulsed wildly, yet the layers upon layers of restraints binding her refused to budge.

The intensity of the pain coursing through her stemmed from the fact that her body was essentially being reassembled from scratch— her ordinary human flesh becoming that of a Genestella. Every cell, from her muscles to her skeleton to her nervous system, was being reborn as a completely different organism.

Unable to pass out or fall asleep due to the drugs administered to her, she was left with no choice but to endure the wrenching pain.

Beyond a wall of tempered glass, Hilda watched with curiosity and excitement, fixing the girl with a devilish grin.

The process continued for days, for weeks, without end.

But it wasn't the pain that made the experience a living hell for Orphelia.

No, it was because of the *power* that had been born in her mind, a force that continued to grow stronger with each passing day. Compared with her fear over what was happening, the pain of being literally torn apart was nothing.

That *power* was proof that she was connected in some way to *the other side*, something that under natural circumstances should never have been brought back here. A fragment of an almighty, merciless, overwhelming divinity. Depending on how that fragment was used, it had the power to accomplish impossible deeds—but at the same time, even the slightest of mistakes risked bringing about irreparable misfortune and ruin.

She didn't want it. She had never wanted such a thing.

It was too much for her to bear. She would have been satisfied in life to possess but a single flower, yet this *thing* was the polar opposite of that.

She wanted to cast it aside, to free herself of it without delay.

If she couldn't, then...

Looking back, the fact that her Strega abilities had manifested as lethal poisons was probably the result of those toxic thoughts.

Of her wish for death.

But that wish wasn't to be.

In the end, she was transformed, and two months after the process had begun, she was returned to the research institute as a Genestella, as a Strega.

Her chestnut-colored hair had turned pure white, her eyes bright red like pieces of ruby—and she had gained unprecedented power. From there, she became Hilda's test subject.

"Kee-hee-hee! Today, we'll be measuring the connection and conversion rates of your mana and the rate of your prana consumption, too!"

"Let's see just how much control you have over your prana! Oh, and we need to confirm the range of toxins you can produce and their flexibility under different intensities! And I know this is somewhat outdated, but let's aim for a fifty percent fatal dose! I'll put in an order for a menagerie of test animals, so we should be able to get started tomorrow! Kee-hee-hee!"

"I see, I see! With that much prana, your flesh can withstand even this level of poison... Wonderful! Theoretically, your body should even be able to withstand a blow from a Lux, so long as it's powered by regular manadite! Then let's increase the output as far as it will go... Oh-ho, are you starting to buckle in there? Well, that can happen when you use an oversized pressure chamber to compress a specific point. Don't worry, just keep going. Our healers are excellent. One or two broken limbs won't matter, not even three!"

"Hmm... Your mental state is a little unstable, isn't it now? I suppose even Stregas of your caliber can't escape the fact that your mental state plays a major role in the potency of your abilities. Then again, it isn't anything that can't be controlled through medication. Now let's continue with the experiments! Today, we're going to be examining the extent of your resistance and its versatility against existing toxins!"

"Now then, today we'll be..."

"Kee-hee-hee!"

....

......

...

Hilda's experiments went on and on and on and on.

One could say that it was those endless trials that made Orphelia the person she was today—a soul composed of grief and resignation. Awakened by the god on *the other side*, nurtured by Hilda, and perfected by the *power* still swelling deep in the back of her mind.

Fate.

It wasn't predestination—at least, not as Orphelia saw it.

For her, fate meant that which had been determined by a greater power.

Those with weak fates had no option but to be enslaved by greater ones.

Having come to this realization, Orphelia's spirit finally found a sense of stability.

If this ruin could even be called *stability*, that is.

Objectively speaking, Hilda conducted her experiments with meticulousness and care.

No matter how overjoyed she might be to have found the perfect specimen, no matter how excited or heated her emotions or how often she might change her mind seemingly on the spur of the moment, she never underestimated the power that had been born inside Orphelia.

Orphelia had been locked away in the deepest part of the research facility, closed off by layer upon layer of corrosion-proof security barriers, each of which was replaced at regular intervals to ensure they didn't break down. All experiments were now conducted remotely, while Orphelia was subject to twenty-four-hour surveillance. A considerable amount of funding had been spent to ensure that no one, Hilda included, needed to come into direct contact with her.

If Hilda had made one mistake, it was in trying to gauge the limits of Orphelia's powers. Of course, that came naturally to a researcher like her. If she didn't know the lower and upper limits of the girl's abilities, she wouldn't be able to attempt to push beyond them.

On this occasion, however, her efforts had resulted in failure.

The reason being there simply *wasn't* a limit to Orphelia's powers.

As a result, she had ended up rampaging out of control.

The inexhaustible supply of mana pouring through the hole in Orphelia's being was converted into prana, which in turn converted the surrounding mana into a toxin that had never before existed anywhere on Earth. This unknown toxin consumed the surrounding equipment, the walls, and the security partitions, eroding them at a terrifying rate.

Nonetheless, Hilda and her team had managed to escape thanks to their many safeguards. If Hilda had underestimated Orphelia's abilities, if she had showed even the slightest carelessness, her fate would have been sealed.

As it was, Orphelia's toxins destroyed the entire laboratory, and the aftermath alone caused the surrounding forest to wither and die and the soil to rot into a poisoned bog.

By the time Orphelia came back to her senses, her surroundings had become a hellscape. Every living thing around her was dead or dying, even inorganic matter was slowly decaying, and the world was filled with the stench of a putrid miasma.

Badly weakened by her outburst of power and on the verge of collapsing into a heap, Orphelia spotted a lone white flower. By some miracle, it still bloomed, as though protected by the melted walls of the research institute.

Half-unaware, she reached out to touch it—but just before her finger could make contact, that small white flower crumbled into dust and scattered to the wind.

*

Dirk Eberwein first encountered the Varda-Vaos shortly after he was brought into Solnage.

At the time, Dirk was highly regarded for his achievements at the Institute, and though he was still only a boy, he was soon made a staff officer at Solnage's military division and entrusted with the planning of operations and the management of his own unit. For Dirk, however, this was but a career stepping stone. He wasn't a Genestella, but he was highly capable and a prime candidate for a future position in the organization's executive ranks.

One day, after returning to his dormitory room, he found a middle-aged man in a nondescript suit waiting for him.

"...Who the hell are you?" he asked dismissively.

"Varda-Vaos," the man answered flatly. He stood alone in the room which otherwise contained only a bed.

"Never heard of you."

There was nothing out of the ordinary about the man's appearance, though something about the way he carried himself suggested that he didn't belong to Solnage. Heck, it wasn't even clear whether the figure was truly human. Among Dirk's most potent weapons were his senses—his powers of observation to see through to a person's innate talents and abilities—but they weren't as effective on this man as they should have been.

No, this figure—Varda—was unmistakably *different* from anyone he had met before.

To have gotten this far through the dormitory's security, they must be fairly powerful. Dirk was just an ordinary human, and had no means of resisting a powerful Genestella.

But Dirk was sure that if the figure wanted to harm him, they would already have done so.

In that case—

"Whaddya want with me?"

"I'm here to recruit you."

"*Recruit* me?" Dirk snorted, sitting down on the bed as he watched Varda from the corner of his eye.

"You despise this world and everything in it, do you not?"

"...Don't talk like you can see right through me. What the hell do you know?"

"Of course I know. Because I am the same."

Dirk knitted his brows at this remark, but quickly realized something.

"You're not a Dante... You're an Orga Lux, aren't you?"

"So you can tell. You're as shrewd as I had hoped," Varda said, unbuttoning their suit jacket.

There, hidden inside, was a huge, unearthly, mechanical-looking necklace.

It was said that Orga Luxes possessed their own sense of will. If that was true, it was within the realm of possibility that they could also act independently. Of course, whether or not you believed such claims was another story.

"Hah… So that's your real body. And? What's this about *recruitment*? What are you trying to get me to do?"

His curiosity had been piqued, even if only a little.

"My associates and I are working on a plan to reshape this world, but we are short on manpower. We need capable, talented individuals, people well-versed in the subtleties of the human mind and in manipulating others."

"A plan to change the world, eh…? How?"

"By bringing about another Invertia."

"What?"

At first, he thought the man was joking or trying to deflect—but their voice was unmistakably serious.

"That would most certainly change things, don't you agree?" Varda asked.

"I guess so…"

Humanity had managed to rebuild after the unprecedented catastrophe of the Invertia—an unprecedented meteor bombardment that had continued for seven days and seven nights—but if the same disaster was to strike again, it would leave society in ruins. Even the IEFs themselves might well be swallowed up by the ensuing chaos.

"What do you think? Are you willing to assist us?"

"…What's in it for me?"

"You hate everything in this world. Is it not reasonable that you would participate in a plan aimed at ending it?" Varda said, as though it was all a matter of course.

"You've got the wrong end of the stick, I think. Yeah, I hate this planet and everything in it, but that doesn't mean I wanna destroy it all," Dirk answered, his voice low and angry as he glowered at Varda. "I just don't wanna lose to what I hate."

Right. That was all there was to it. He didn't even care about winning.

He just didn't want to lose. *That* was the only reason he kept living.

He hated his parents, whose faces he couldn't even remember. He hated the Institute that had made him what he was today, and he hated all its staff, too. He hated the foundations that treated the whole of society like their personal property. He hated Genestella and the untold possibilities they represented. He hated ordinary people clutching desperately to their antiquated values. He hated arrogant winners and miserable, pathetic losers alike. He hated the fools who misjudged their own powers and failed to show restraint, and he hated the idiots left with no other choice but to reduce themselves to flattery and groveling. He hated the incompetent and the useless. He hated people's contemptuous kindness and their strictness that did nothing but injure. He hated their sugary, sentimental love. Animals, plants, beautiful scenery, colors, nature, the food that tasted like sand in his mouth, the sleep that brought nothing but nightmares, his abominable past, his cursed future, men, women, adults, children, the elderly, himself, and every last thing on the face of this planet—he hated the lot of them.

Each was just as odious as the next, and he despised them all in equal measure.

"I see. Perhaps I was mistaken?" Varda murmured, their voice devoid of emotion.

"No. It's a pain having to admit it, but you're basically right on the money."

"Oh?"

"I'll hear you out. Let's see if your little birdsong can catch my interest, Orga Lux."

And so Dirk was brought on board with the plans of Varda and their associates.

That said, their scheme to cause a second Invertia was already in its final stages when Dirk joined the group. He was to receive information necessary to carrying out their plans through Varda, which he would then examine and improve—that was the extent of his role.

On the whole, their scheme was both astonishingly elaborate and appallingly sloppy. After a while, he came to a realization—the individuals involved with this plan had an unbelievably naive understanding of human psychology. Or rather, they simply had no interest in comprehending the human mind.

Dirk was convinced that was why they had reached out to recruit him: to lean on his abilities to make up for their own inadequacies. The power to make people act, to make them kneel, to make them give up and surrender. To him, those were all second nature.

Dirk hadn't personally visited the site where the plan was to be initiated, but perhaps out of recognition of his work, or maybe because he had gained their trust, he was finally able to meet the ringleaders just before it was to be executed.

The central figure behind the effort was a boy named Ecknardt, who like Varda, was clearly not a human being. He was a visitor from *the other side*, a slice of a greater power. If manadite was the crystalline form of mana, and urm-manadite was the same but of a higher purity, then Ecknardt was something beyond that—the ultimate urm-manadite that required neither exterior armor nor mechanical apparatuses. He could, in other words, operate entirely on his own, without the help of human hands. In Varda's words, he was *a terminal of the divine, restored from mana*.

Next came Madiath Mesa, a former winner of the Phoenix who now served as a member of the Festa Executive Committee. Dirk recognized him at first glance and took an instant disliking to him. Of course, there wasn't a thing in this world that he *did* like, but he took a particular *dis*like to Madiath. The man went around with a friendly smile always plastered on his face, but beneath that mask burned a blaze of pure wrath.

Nonetheless, the plan was soon foiled—by none other than Haruka Amagiri.

Ecknardt vanished without a trace, and Madiath and the others were forced to set about replanning from scratch.

And then...

*   *   *

Dirk's presence in Lieseltania that day was ultimately a coincidence. His unit had just completed a separate operation and was on standby at a base in the small city-state when the order came in to monitor and investigate a research laboratory owned by Frauenlob. According to their intel, security had recently been increased considerably, with a large number of autonomous puppets and automatic weapon systems having been deployed.

Given that the laboratory hadn't directly increased its security personnel, they were most likely conducting experiments of a particularly sensitive nature. Lieseltania was extraterritorial, so the IEFs were free to do whatever they liked there. Dirk figured it was just some pet-project experiment, but this was a direct order, and work was work, so he stationed surveillance personnel around the complex. He was just beginning to gather information when the incident occurred.

"...What?"

"It's destroyed! Completely destroyed! The whole lab...! We were able to confirm a helicopter leaving—the staff have taken flight...! Huh...?! I-impossible...! Th-there's a monster here! Arrrggghhh!"

The choppy call was interrupted by a rush of panicked voices and a volley of gunfire, before cutting off abruptly.

Deeming the mission unimportant, Dirk had sent a rookie to keep tabs on the laboratory, but that seemed now to have backfired. The personnel he had assigned to other locations weren't picking up, and the data feeds from the various instruments they had deployed had likewise fallen silent.

Safe in his command vehicle, he folded his arms and immediately set to thinking.

If that final report was true, then the laboratory had already been destroyed and the staff were gone, no doubt having fled to Frauenlob's Lieseltania base of operations. Given their location, it would be some time before they could dispatch any rescue or investigative units to the area.

Besides, the last words of that call had caught his attention.

"If I can get ahead of them here..."

He divided his forces into two groups, sending the first to investigate the laboratory itself and the second to seal off the surrounding area. Fortunately, he was well within his rights to exercise his authority within Lieseltania. He was clearly acting of his own accord, but management wouldn't complain so long as he styled his actions as a rescue mission or something of the sort.

The images from the small, unmanned reconnaissance aircraft he had dispatched did indeed show that the laboratory had been devastated. Nonetheless, it wasn't long before the connection was lost and the visual feed dropped off. It seemed the mana levels in the surrounding area had temporarily dropped, causing the lost connection. Could that be why the rookie's call to him had abruptly cut off, too?

Considering the possibility of a biohazard situation, he notified his team to equip special protective equipment and to carry old-fashioned radios that didn't rely on meteoric engineering.

After a while, reports started to come in: first data on the atmospheric conditions as measured by the team's equipment, and then—

"There's a woman here, standing in the middle of it all."

The team that he had sent to investigate was made up of veterans, unlike his choice of surveillance. But even so, Dirk could still hear the confusion in their voices, impossible to fully conceal.

"A woman? Explain."

"That's..."

Unable to get an answer to his question, Dirk clicked his tongue and stepped out from the command vehicle.

He wasn't the type to directly involve himself with operations in the field. Unlike the other members of his unit, he was just an ordinary human. On top of that, he had little in the way of combat training and wasn't very athletic.

But this time, he wanted to see what was happening for himself. He didn't quite know why. It was just a gut feeling. He normally thought of himself as a creature of logic, but he still recognized the importance of intuition. People weren't machines. After all, without understanding the emotions that drove people to make irrational decisions, it would be impossible to manipulate them.

When he arrived at the scene, he could see the surprise in his masked subordinates' eyes. Nonetheless, they silently opened a path for him.

In the center of that hellscape, with everything rotting around him and a strange odor burning his nostrils, he did indeed find a young woman standing there, just as reported. Instantly, every hair on his body stood on end and a cold sweat poured from his forehead in torrents.

It seemed the rookie wasn't mistaken.

This was undeniably a monster.

His squad members surrounded the girl with their guns at the ready, but Dirk raised a hand to restrain them.

"But, boss..."

"Stand back, you hear me? Don't tell me you haven't caught on yet? If she wanted, she could have slaughtered the lot of us a dozen times over by now."

"...!"

His troops looked indignant at this remark, but did as Dirk instructed and lowered their weapons, falling back a few steps.

"...Hey," Dirk called out.

The girl slowly turned her crimson eyes his way. In her gaze, he saw resignation and sadness deeper than any he had witnessed before.

"What are you?"

"Me...? I'm...Orphelia. Orphelia Landlufen." Her voice was flat and indifferent, yet at the same time replete with desolation.

"Are you responsible for this mess?"

"...Yes. I don't really remember it all, but it must have been me," Orphelia whispered, casting her gaze over her surroundings.

She looked exhausted, on the verge of collapsing.

"Oh… Were those people who attacked me earlier your friends…? It was all so sudden, and I… They're still alive, at least. I think."

"Hmph. That's not what I'm here for. From what you're saying, I'm guessing you didn't mean to do all this?"

"…I don't want to do anything anymore."

"Oh?" Dirk said, his eyes narrowing.

This, he realized, could very well be the opportunity of a lifetime.

"Yes… This must be my fate."

"Hmph. *Fate*?" Dirk scoffed.

He, of course, didn't believe in such a thing. *Fate* was no more than the ramblings of fools who had given up on thinking for themselves.

And yet…

"So you're saying you were just going along with your *fate* here?"

"…"

At that moment, Orphelia's eyes met his for the first time.

Until that moment, though she had been looking at him, she hadn't *seen* him. It was fair to say she had responded to his words only by reflex.

But this was different.

"Okay, Orphelia. It's not like I've got any sympathy for you, but I *understand* you. You wanna follow your *fate*, am I right?"

"…Follow my…fate…," she mumbled, repeating his words.

"In that case, come with me. I'll give you the freedom to follow this fate of yours," he said, fixing her with a glare.

"I wonder… Are you—is your fate strong enough for that?" Orphelia murmured quizzically, almost to herself. Then a long plume of gray gas, like the hand of a wraith, rose up from her feet and loomed before his eyes.

His troops all lifted their weapons, but Dirk raised a hand once more to urge restraint.

"Who cares? *I* don't believe in fate. Still…" He paused there, staring at the thin tendrils that could no doubt kill him with the slightest touch. "I'll accept it, for your sake. All of it. Even if you end up taking thousands, millions of lives some day in the future, I'll accept that it was your fate."

"…!" Orphelia's eyes widened.

Here was a woman who had given up on everything, who had resigned herself to grief. Dirk could tell all this just by looking into her eyes. From his point of view, the decision was an easy one.

But at the same time, Orphelia possessed a horrifying power. Even at the Institute, packed as it was with so many prodigious talents, he had never before seen a Strega of her caliber. Not even the most elite units of the foundations were in possession of someone as gifted as her.

Perhaps Orphelia was still struggling to come to terms with her overwhelming power. Considering the devastation around her, that was little wonder.

It was also as clear as day that she fundamentally abhorred this power she called *fate*.

That being the case, the easiest solution was just to accept it all, exactly the way it was.

No matter what happened in the future, no matter what she might do with her powers, he would accept that it wasn't Orphelia who was responsible but rather the fate that had ensnared her.

That was her only possible escape route from a future of depravity and irresponsibility.

And he was the devil, offering her a deal.

"…" Orphelia watched Dirk in silence for a long moment before she averted her gaze in apparent exhaustion. "All right. What are you going to do?"

With that, she accepted the devil's hand.

"I'm going to remake this shithole world. So first, come with me to Asterisk."

"Asterisk…?"

"You look like you're around school-age, right? You're definitely not any older than twenty, I'm guessing? That'll do, then."

Dirk himself had decided to enroll at Le Wolfe Black Institute starting the following spring.

That offer included the position of student council president.

Le Wolfe had been unable to control the campus and the Rotlicht entertainment district for some time, and while a lack of restraint masquerading as freedom and the individual power it nurtured was part of the school's core values, the place was of little use to Solnage if it remained completely disorganized. Dirk had been entrusted with the task of reestablishing control.

"I see... If that's my fate, then so be it."

"With your help, I'll be able to draw up a new plan. It'll be much easier to get things done with you as student council president rather than some Solnage pawn."

Le Wolfe's student council president had the right to appoint the school's highest-ranked Page One. Whenever one president's term of office expired, the top place was always given to the next one's choice.

"First things first, I'll need to solidify my position. Then I'll gradually introduce you to the others."

Already, Dirk had put together the bare bones of an idea.

It might not have been as grand or as organized as the plan for which Varda had recruited him—to bring about a second Invertia— but so long as the goal was achieved, nothing else really mattered.

Certainly, with both Orphelia's and Varda's power at their disposal, it wasn't out of reach, and with Madiath and Dirk's positions, the groundwork was in place. Finally, Asterisk would make the perfect stage for their show.

After all, Dirk absolutely despised that godforsaken miniature garden of a city.

CHAPTER 3
ODD EYE

"Whoa, so they're finally making a move…?"

Eishirou Yabuki murmured under his breath. He had been nibbling on a rice ball with his left hand and peering through binoculars with his right. As he spoke, he licked the last grains from his fingers.

It was the middle of the night, past three o'clock in the morning, and he was stationed on the elevated monorail that ran across Asterisk's perimeter. In the darkness, with no light shining from the moon or stars to illuminate his surroundings, he followed closely as a car emerged from the grounds of Le Wolfe Black Institute. From its make, model, and plate number, he could tell it was the vehicle reserved for the student council president's exclusive use—in other words, Dirk was undoubtedly inside. From this distance, it might have made sense for him to use his far-sight techniques to keep tabs on what was happening, but at night it was easier just to rely on machines and equipment.

"All righty, then. This will probably be my last chance. I'd better get myself together."

Eishirou leaped down from the overpass and set off in pursuit of the car, his eyes never leaving his target. As a Genestella, he should have little difficulty keeping up—so long, of course, as the vehicle didn't take off at high speed. Fortunately, it soon entered the redevelopment area not far from the campus. Under the cover of darkness, jumping from ruin to ruin, he continued his pursuit while maintaining a solid distance.

His current mission, as issued by Claudia, was to secure proof that Dirk was in fact a member of the Golden Bough Alliance. Ideally, he would like to catch him meeting up with either Madiath Mesa (going by his alias Lamina Mortis) or the Varda-Vaos, both of whom had already gone into hiding.

Of course, as was to be expected, Dirk was an incredibly cautious individual, and until now he had offered up no leads for Eishirou to hone in on. He seldom set foot outside of Le Wolfe, and even when he did, it was difficult to tail or track him successfully without the necessary manpower. Eishirou, operating alone after having been instructed not to rely on other Shadowstar agents, was severely limited in what he could actually do. On top of that, Dirk always had members of Grimalkin attached to him as his personal security. When dealing with the best intelligence agency of Asterisk's six schools, caution was always the wisest course of action.

As such, until this moment, he had been unable to achieve any solid results, simply biding his time as he awaited his opportunity.

He didn't know what kind of plans the Golden Bough Alliance was pursuing, but the larger their ambitions, the more they would need to communicate through face-to-face meetings. Sinodomius's intelligence network had eyes throughout Asterisk, so no matter how carefully you conducted a conversation through a mobile terminal or communication device, you could never completely dismiss the possibility that someone might intercept it. Short remote conversations might avoid detection, but once they stretched beyond a certain duration, they could be intercepted by the Orga Lux known as the Eye of Providence. It was dangerous to use even the student council president's direct hotline for more than the briefest of communications.

"Ah...!"

After passing through the Rotlicht into an area filled with nothing but dilapidated ruins, the black car stopped at a street corner in the redevelopment area. Eishirou monitored the surrounding vicinity, but he couldn't sense anyone else nearby.

What the...?

As he stared breathlessly at the vehicle from the roof of a crumbling building, the rear passenger door suddenly swung open.

The first to emerge was a man who looked to be a bodyguard, followed by Dirk Eberwein, the Tyrant himself. As Dirk climbed out from the car, the bodyguard whispered something in his ear, and he immediately swung his piercing gaze in Eishirou's direction.

Uh-oh! No way...?!

Startled, he turned around to retreat, at least for the time being, when—

"Hey, you. The one from Shadowstar."

In the moonless dark, a man had appeared behind him.

"..." Eishirou was speechless.

For a ninja, suppressing one's own presence while detecting others took precedence over all other techniques. The essence of ninjutsu wasn't in fighting or assassination nor even in your own clan's special abilities, but rather in stealth. Even Eishirou, who had been practicing ninjutsu for as long as he could remember, still considered stealth his particular specialty.

And yet—

"Color me surprised. I never would have thought someone could get the jump on me," Eishirou said with a forced smile. As he spoke, he leaped back to put some distance between himself and the newcomer.

"Oh no, cheer up. Even I wasn't able to get any closer than this. You're the real thing, you know?" the man said with a laid-back laugh, notably out of place given the circumstances.

He looked to be a little over twenty years old, with dull blond hair and a thin mustache. His face was well-defined, but he had an air of laziness about him highlighted by his sleepy eyes. At first glance, he seemed like the kind of young man you could find just about anywhere.

"And you are…? I mean, you seem to know who *I* am already."

Eishirou was certainly no stranger to being tailed. That was simply what happened when you trained with a superior partner, such as his father Bujinsai.

Yet this time, he had taken care to monitor his surroundings— and there had been absolutely no sign of anyone.

In other words, the man in front of him now must be at the same level as his father—or perhaps even a step above.

"I don't really care for names. I'm in the same line of work as you, though," the man said, pulling a Lux activation body from the holder at his waist.

Did that make him a member of Grimalkin, then?

"Hey, hey, at least make it look like you're putting in an effort. I hate the way you Cats are always so hotheaded," Eishirou said, carefully measuring his timing as he readied his kunai knives. "Given the situation…I'm guessing I was set up, huh?"

"You've been watching my boss for a while now, haven't you? I told you to leave us alone, but you just had to keep getting in the way." The man activated a claw-shaped Lux on his left hand.

Is that…Arachne's Thread?

Arachne's Thread was an Orga Lux in the possession of Le Wolfe Black Institute, capable of creating and manipulating invisible threads from the tips of its claws. It wasn't particularly powerful, but it could deliver nasty surprises.

"Heh. So Grimalkin's putting on a special show just for me? I guess I should be honored. So…are you with the Gold Eyes or the Silver Eyes?"

The agents who worked for Grimalkin were organized into two broad groups—the Silver Eyes, which were mostly active on campus, and the Gold Eyes, which operated off campus. Given that this confrontation was taking place away from Le Wolfe, Eishirou's assailant most likely belonged to the latter group. However, escort operations were apparently under the jurisdiction of the Silver Eyes, so if he had come with Dirk, that possibility couldn't be ruled out. In general, the Gold Eyes had greater fighting abilities, but...

Eishirou didn't expect an answer to these questions. He was simply buying time to reassess his situation, to confirm whether there were any other soldiers in the vicinity waiting to ambush him, and to plan his next moves. No foe would be foolish enough to provide their quarry with information when they intended to kill them in short order.

And yet—

"Me? I'm with both."

"Huh?"

"I said I'm with the Gold Eyes *and* the Silver Eyes. Which tends to keep me pretty busy. That asshole thinks it's okay to call me whenever he's got a problem," the man said with a weary sigh.

"...Seriously?"

Eishirou was taken aback by how readily his counterpart had responded to him, but it was this new information that froze him in place.

"So...you're the current Odd Eye, then?"

Only Grimalkin's best agent at any given time was listed as a member of both the Gold Eyes and the Silver Eyes. In other words, this was the most capable agent of Asterisk's most capable intelligence agency—the one known by the code name Odd Eye.

And now, Eishirou was facing off against him.

"I guess that must make you Baldanders, then?"

After Orphelia Landlufen as Erenshkigal and Hyougo Arayashiki as Ruffian, Odd Eye was the third-most powerful student at Le Wolfe. His alias had been circulating through the underworld for some time now, but his face and true identity remained unknown, and so there were more than a few who questioned his very existence.

"Ah. You seem pretty clued in."

"Not at all. If I'd never heard of you in this business, I'd deserve to be let go." Eishirou responded casually, but he couldn't deny that his forehead had broken out into a cold sweat. Inwardly, he was at a total loss.

The situation could hardly be any worse. To start with, his mission had ended up being a complete failure, then he had managed to get himself baited into this trap, and now the most powerful operative of an enemy faction meant to take his life.

To be perfectly honest, he *was* confident in his skills.

He had once taken out Gold Eye Number Seven, so even against another Cat, he should have been able to stand his ground. But Baldanders was another matter entirely. Of course, it was always possible that his adversary was bluffing, but Eishirou could see well enough that the defenses of the man in front of him were impeccable. Whether or not he actually was Baldanders, it was obvious that Eishirou was outclassed.

I guess it's time for plan thirty-six... This could get messy...

But the moment Eishirou decided to take a step back, a sudden chill ran down his spine.

"...!"

Reflexively, he stopped in his tracks and looked around. At first glance, there was no sign of any visible change. But Eishirou had already made one mistake. Keeping his gaze fixed on Baldanders, he meticulously sharpened his five senses and finally recognized that something was indeed off.

It was the sound.

The sound of the wind blowing through the air was different than usual—a discrepancy so slight that it would have gone undetected by any ordinary person.

He quickly removed his jacket—every item of his clothing and equipment was designed to be easily removable—and threw it behind him.

The jacket danced in the night wind, but instead of being carried away or falling to the ground, it hung there in place, as though caught by something.

"...I see. I wondered why you were wasting your time chatting, but I guess you were using the opportunity to run those invisible threads around me, huh?"

As an Orga Lux, Arachne's Thread and its ability to manipulate highly sticky and invisible strings wasn't well-suited to hand-to-hand combat. For that reason, it was rarely seen at the Festa, and the other schools lacked detailed information on its specifications. Eishirou knew of its capabilities, but he hadn't expected it to be able to entrap him so quickly.

Judging from the sound and the way that the wind was moving, his foe must have already deployed a spider's web of threads around him. No doubt the reason he hadn't ensnared him directly was to avoid tipping him off ahead of time.

It would be difficult to cut through threads produced by an Orga Lux via regular means, but even so, Eishirou doubted they would pose a problem so long as he was only caught by one or two of them. After all, he could always remove an article of clothing as necessary, or even scrape off a little skin if one got caught on his body. As such, for the Orga Lux to be put to maximum effect, it would need to deploy several layers before its quarry could be rendered immobile.

By revealing his identity now, Baldanders was trying to prompt him to choose retreat. Eishirou's objective—to pursue Dirk and obtain evidence of his involvement—was already foiled, and there was no point in fighting an opponent like Odd Eye here. Under any other circumstances, he would indeed have chosen to fall back.

But Baldanders had anticipated all that, and he had set his trap accordingly.

"Huh? You've got a pretty good intuition there," Baldanders said, his expression bored as he scratched his head. "What a pain in the ass."

Without even pausing to catch his breath, Eishirou rushed forward, closing the distance between him and his opponent.

This should do it...!

A powerful attack attempting to catch his foe off guard, a main-stay of the Yabuki clan's repertoire.

Even Baldanders ought to have had a tough time dealing with the Void Tide technique.

And yet…

"Oops…!"

"…!"

Before the dark kunai blade that seemed to melt into the night could reach its target, Baldanders's right hand, which until then had been scratching his head, was suddenly gripping a musket gun, the muzzle pressed against Eishirou's flank.

Even though Eishirou had clearly moved faster than his opponent, Baldanders had still managed to surpass him. In other words, they were simply incomparable. Eishirou prided himself on his fleetness of foot and his sharp eyes, but even he hadn't been able to catch his foe pulling out the weapon.

Then, like a high-pitched bale of laughter, a gunshot rang out.

A jet-black bullet pierced Eishirou's flesh—and at the same moment, his body collapsed into a heap of leaves. At least, that was how it must have looked to Baldanders.

"Heh, so that's your *hiding-in-the-leaves* technique, I take it? I've never seen a Yabuki clan trick firsthand before." The young man watched with one eyebrow raised, apparently impressed.

"…Not really. I don't actually have anywhere to go from here. This is like a waking nightmare."

With a grimace, Eishirou returned to his position of just a moment ago. He couldn't begin to determine where his foe had deployed other threads. While Ayato could use his *shiki* ability to get an all but perfect grasp of any situation, Eishirou could only make predictions based on the movements and sound of the wind.

No. He *did* have one more move up his sleeve.

"Anyway… Can you explain that thing for me?"

In his hands, Baldanders was wielding what looked like a musket-type Lux.

No. Eishirou stopped himself. That was no ordinary Lux. It was an Orga Lux.

"This thing? I'm sure you've heard of it. It's the Gremlin Barrett," Baldanders said with a swing of the gun.

Of course, Eishirou was familiar with the name. Instead of propelling a projectile directly into the target's body, the Gremlin Barrett unleashed bullets designed to temporarily disrupt their sense of balance. Like Arachne's Thread, it was another of Le Wolfe's Orga Luxes, and because the cost it extracted from its users was relatively light, this one did appear in the Festa with some frequency.

That, however, wasn't the problem right now.

The main principle behind the distribution of Orga Luxes was that each could have only a single user, and each user could wield only a single Orga Lux. There were occasions when certain individuals made use of multiple weapons, but even then, they were limited to using a single Orga Lux in conjunction with regular Luxes. Eishirou had never before heard of anyone being able to wield two separate Orga Luxes.

The reason that Dantes and Stregas were incompatible with Orga Luxes was that the weapons tended to be particularly sensitive to other powers. And for the same reason, they were also incompatible with other Orga Luxes.

And yet...

So he's using Arachne's Thread with his left hand and the Gremlin Barrett with his right...?

It was hard to believe that this foe could be compatible with *two* Orga Luxes, but the effects of Arachne's Thread didn't appear to have dissipated. In other words, Baldanders was somehow using the Gremlin Barrett at the same time. He wasn't simply switching between the two—he was wielding them simultaneously.

That was even more difficult to accept.

This is insane... But I can hardly deny what's happening in front of my own eyes, can I?

Eishirou immediately brought his stray thoughts under control and gave his wrist a slight flick.

All of a sudden, a gust of wind broke out, and the fallen leaves scattered by his earlier transformation technique were thrown into the air.

Then, within a split second, they froze in place, each of them hooked by invisible threads.

I can't go up and I can't go back… So my only way out is through him?

Thanks to those leaves, he had a rough idea of the locations of the threads. Spiderwebs typically relied on branches and leaves to serve as anchor points, but Arachne's Thread could hang its string on empty air. The abandoned building was already enshrouded by a dome of threads, with only the back section toward Baldanders remaining open—and that too would no doubt be filled in before too long. Looking carefully, Eishirou could see his foe's left hand moving slightly, no doubt busy extending more threads.

The longer he waited, the fewer options he would have.

"Heh. I guess it's time for the next one."

While Eishirou's feet were burning with impatience, Baldanders calmly swapped the Gremlin Barrett in his left hand for another inactive Lux.

"…How about Zelus's Bell?"

A third Orga Lux. This time, Eishirou wasn't surprised. He didn't know what kind of gimmick his foe was using, but there could be no doubt that he was fully capable of wielding multiple Orga Luxes at the same time.

The rust-colored bell, shaped like the face of a corpse on the cusp of breaking out into a wail, had similar characteristics to the Lyre-Poros held by Queenvale Academy.

In other words, it worked by attacking with sound.

Though not as powerful as the Lyre-Poros, the shattering sonic waves produced by Zelus's Bell rang out in all directions, leaving no area uncovered. Like the Arachne's Thread and the Gremlin Barret, it wasn't a particularly powerful Orga Lux, but it would be a major nuisance.

"...Just how many Orga Luxes do you have?"

"Why don't you take a guess?"

Without answering Eishirou's question, Baldanders shook his right hand—and at that moment, the air around him quivered with a low, earth-rumbling moan.

"Ngh...!"

Sound waves strong enough to distort space tore through Eishirou's skin, making his bones creak from the pressure.

Nonetheless, it was still tolerable. The power of Zelus's Bell increased with proximity, and likewise decreased as you moved farther away. At the moment, the distance between Eishirou and his opponent was less than five meters. The crushing sound wave might have made for an impossible-to-dodge ranged attack, but it shouldn't prove fatal at this distance.

Even so, the damage could build up with successive strikes. If he moved too far, he risked getting caught by the threads—still, he did his best to put more distance between the two of them.

The next moment—

"Huh...?"

All of a sudden, the air around him distorted, and Eishirou found himself having fallen to the ground.

He wasted no time trying to rise to his feet, but he stumbled, unable to fully stand.

He could still summon his strength, so the problem wasn't with his limbs.

"Is this...?"

Paralysis of his sense of balance—probably the result of the Gremlin Barrett.

But he thought he had completely evaded the last attack. Then why...?

"How's that for you? The Gremlin Barret and Zelus's Bell work pretty good together, eh?" Baldanders explained.

Eishirou's skin erupted in a frigid sweat.

He could hardly believe it.

It wasn't supposed to be possible.

"...Y-you combined...the abilities...of two Orga Luxes...?"

Not only was he in possession of multiple Orga Luxes.

Not only was he capable of wielding them all at the same time.

To top it all off, he was able to *combine* their effects into one...

In other words, he had merged the sonic attack of Zelus's Bell with the Gremlin Barrett's ability to temporarily paralyze its target's sense of balance.

"You've got to be kidding me...," Eishirou gasped in disbelief.

"Well then, we might as well get this over with... Unfortunately, I don't have an Orga Lux on hand that can attack at long range, though."

With those words, Baldanders deactivated Zelus's Bell and swapped it for a large-caliber gun-type Lux instead.

"It's just a regular old Lux, but it's modified to boost its power level. One shot at a vital organ, and down you go," he said, pointing the muzzle at Eishirou as the manadite core began to glow.

"N-ngh...!"

Eishirou managed to pull himself up on his elbows, but his vision was blurry, his balance unsteady, and he fell flat on his face.

In his current state, he wouldn't be able to avoid an oncoming attack... Unless—

"See ya, then."

Just before the man across from him pulled the trigger and a high-powered bullet of light shot out, Eishirou stretched his arms, leaped up into the air with a spin, and landed firmly on his feet.

"Ugh..."

"Whoa, dangerous stuff!"

The dizziness was still somewhat present, but it disappeared as soon as he raised a hand to his head and applied a final adjustment.

"Interesting... So you used your Void Tide technique on *yourself*?

Must be pretty convenient." Deactivating his Lux, Baldanders rubbed his chin.

Was it that obvious...? And how the hell does he even know *about my Void Tide techniques?!*

But the man was exactly right.

Eishirou's clan had passed down their Void Tide techniques for eons, since a time before mana existed in the world (or to be more precise, when it existed only in extremely limited concentrations). They could only be employed by those whose Yabuki blood ran strong. The effects were varied, but in general they interfered with the mental and physical statuses of the target.

That said, the techniques didn't affect a target directly. Normal humans aside, Genestella were highly resistant to brainwashing and other forms of mental interference, which tended to have only weak effects on them. Moreover, given that his clan's Void Tide techniques had been developed during an age when mana remained scarce, it was quite impossible for them to exert a direct influence on the target.

For that reason, they functioned not by directly affecting the target's mind or body, but rather by utilizing the instincts and reflexes innate to human physiology. For example, people tended to unconsciously avoid certain colors, shapes, sounds, smells, or combinations thereof. Reflexively, they sought to dispel those things they found intrinsically unpleasant or uncanny. His clan's Void Tide techniques worked by projecting such images onto the subject, and as a result, prompting certain thoughts or movements. The Yabuki clan's wards used to keep people at a distance were just another application of the same principle.

But while these techniques couldn't manipulate people directly, they were useful for deflecting attacks and slowing a target's evasive movements. For a ninja, that was typically enough.

This time, Eishirou had forced his body to ignore its paralysis and leap up by applying the technique to himself.

"Well, I don't think anyone else could have pulled off that trick!" he laughed as he rubbed the bottom of his nose in satisfaction.

In fact, the reason he had managed to abscond from his village without punishment was that he had such an extremely high aptitude for these kinds of Void Tide techniques. He was proud to say in that regard, he had even surpassed his father, his other ninja skills and abilities notwithstanding.

"Ah... I was wondering why you didn't try to get closer, but it looks like you already know about my Void Tide techniques, huh? Full points to you, I guess."

The best way to kill one's target without fail would be to aim at their neck or heart with a melee weapon.

And yet, Baldanders had made no attempt to close the distance.

No doubt he was guarding against Eishirou's Void Tide techniques. They were, after all, known for being able to turn the tables even on superior opponents.

"You know what they say—a wise man never courts danger. Cowardice is the key to a long life, don't you think?"

Eishirou could agree with that sentiment. In this business, you had to be a coward to survive.

After all, fights between two special operatives were the complete opposite of public performances like the Festa. In such spectacles, the objective was to clash with all one's strength, constantly butting against one's foe and employing all the techniques and abilities at one's disposal. But in his world, the best course of action was to eliminate your opponent before they were aware of your existence— and if that proved impossible, the key was to win without taking a blow.

Just as Baldanders was doing to Eishirou right now.

"But if it's come to this, I guess I'm gonna have to double down and finish you off here. I didn't really want to have to use this one... but I guess I've got no choice, eh?"

With those words, Baldanders retrieved another deactivated Orga Lux.

What on earth was it...?

"Uh-oh..."

Eishirou's face contorted as his eyes lit up with recognition.

With his right hand, his foe activated a club with an urm-manadite tip.

"The Wolt-Moon," Eishirou all but spat.

Among the various Orga Luxes held by Le Wolfe Black Institute, the Wolt-Moon was among the most malignant, surpassing even the Raksha-Nada. That club, created by Ladislav Bartošik himself, possessed the ability of *decomposition*—an astonishing power to reduce practically anything it touched to ashes.

But as notorious as it was, in actual combat, it wasn't a particularly practical weapon.

The Wolt-Moon reduced any object it struck to dust, but it only worked if it could physically touch the target. If it made contact with someone's clothes, it would be those pieces of fabric that would be destroyed first. And that *decomposition* ability could only be used a limited number of times. Unlike, for example, the Pan-Dora, its total uses couldn't be restored once exhausted, and so under certain conditions, it would be rendered nothing more than an unwieldy, blunt instrument.

Because of the high cost it required from its user, its remarkably low compatibility rate, and most of all, its utter brutality (it decomposed human bodies, too), it had appeared in the Festa only once. Afterward, it had gained notoriety in the underworld as a weapon used by Le Wolfe's most ruthless thugs.

"So you've brought another nasty toy..."

Like the Four Colored Runeswords, this was another weapon impossible to defend against. Fortunately, its reach was rather short.

Moreover, the Wolt-Moon could only be used in close quarters, which gave Eishirou a chance to come out on top.

But with that thought, he stopped himself.

No, why would someone who calls himself a coward, who's kept his distance up till now, change tactics so easily...?

At that moment, a second possibility dawned on him: combined abilities.

"...! No way...!"

With a light tap, Baldanders brought the Wolt-Moon in his right hand up to Arachne's Thread in his left.

A second later, the abandoned building that Eishirou and his adversary were standing atop decomposed without leaving so much as a trace.

"Shit...!"

But before it could hit the ground, Eishirou's falling body came to a sudden stop in midair.

His foe's invisible threads, it seemed, had caught him.

"...I didn't think you'd laced those threads through the inside of the building, too... You got me...," he murmured from his position in a hammock-like net, glancing at Baldanders standing now a few meters down below.

So I can't move either leg, my back, or my left arm at all... Looks like I can budge my head and my right arm a little, though...

He tried to calmly take in the situation, but objectively speaking, it was now practically hopeless.

"So you combined the abilities of the Wolt-Moon and Arachne's Thread, I take it?"

Disassembling everything that was in direct contact with those unseen threads, and throwing him headfirst into the middle of a trap...

Fortunately, even ensnared like this, at no point was his skin in direct contact with the threads. Even if the Wolt-Moon's ability was triggered yet again, it would be his clothes that decomposed first.

Still, if this same maneuver was used two, maybe three times in a row, he would be done for—though Eishirou suspected that his foe wouldn't want to use up his limited stock so easily. After all, Baldanders had for all intents and purposes already won.

If I could get out of my clothes... No, that wouldn't work. Even if I did manage to wriggle out, at this rate...

The dust from the decomposed building drifted through the surrounding area, faintly highlighting the invisible threads. Those threads, stretched out in a dozen or so layers in every possible direction, completely encircled him.

"I wonder?"

Despite all this, there was no change in Baldanders's expression. Even now, he seemed neither alert nor gloating, his eyes displaying only the same lethargy that had filled them from the beginning of their encounter.

"But...I've learned one thing. Looks like you don't have total freedom combining the abilities of your Orga Luxes, do you?"

"..."

Without responding, Baldanders returned the Wolt-Moon to its holder and retrieved his gun-type Lux. As Eishirou had suspected, he didn't want to waste the Orga Lux's limited uses.

"I'm right, aren't I? There ought to be more effective Orga Luxes to combine with the Wolt-Moon. But seeing as you aren't trying anything like that...I'm guessing there's some kind of compatibility problem, right?"

"...This time, it's over," Baldanders declared, his voice devoid of emotion as he pointed his gun straight at Eishirou.

"Yep, it's over," Eishirou responded with a slight grin.

The next moment—a red line ran across Baldanders's neck, from which a plume of blood burst forth.

"...?! What...?!"

For the first time, Baldanders's expression was one of utmost shock as he raised his hands to the gash, yet he was unable to stem the bleeding.

"Heh-heh...! Right by the skin of my teeth, huh?"

Eishirou was making a V sign with his right hand, which he had just thrown forward with all his might.

Yes—he had just cast a *shuriken* to tear through Baldanders's neck.

"Impossible... But there was no sign, no indication...!"

Baldanders swayed unsteadily. The *shuriken* used by the Yabuki clan were produced from a reaction of one's own blood with a special medium, and they were designed to gouge right through the flesh of their target in such a way that it was difficult to stem the bleeding.

"Well, that's on you. We've both got our own special ways of hiding our own presence. Don't beat yourself up over it. There's no way you could have noticed."

"...Another...Void Tide...technique...?"

Baldanders was clearly unable to grasp what had just happened, but Eishirou responded with silence.

He wasn't stupid enough to go out of his way to reveal his secrets, though his foe's assumption had indeed been in the ballpark.

Baldanders, on alert against Eishirou's Void Tide techniques, had maintained a fixed distance from his quarry. At that range, there was enough of a power differential that he would be able to resist any tricks that Eishirou might try to pull against him. Naturally, there was no way that he would have fallen victim to a mere thrown weapon.

Unless, of course, another Void Tide technique was put to use.

The Yabuki possessed a wide variety of such moves. Among them was the immobilizing technique used by Bujinsai that made its target's body freeze with tension.

The one that Eishirou had used this time was his own original technique, one he had named the Fivefold Seal. To put it simply, its purpose was to create an opening for him to attack, much like many regular Void Tide techniques. The difference was in its level of accuracy.

The Fivefold Seal worked by shutting off all five of its target's senses, even if only for a brief moment. Regular Void Tide techniques might be able to cut off Baldanders's sight for a few seconds—but that wouldn't be enough to defeat him. Though it might slow him down, so long as his other senses continued to function, it would be impossible to disrupt his sense of *continuity*. There was a famous story of an old master who had been able to respond to assailants even in his sleep so long as he kept one or two of his senses on high alert at all times.

So what was the solution? The answer was simple: to shut down *all* of the target's senses. Then there would be a complete blank in their sense of continuity.

The problem was that Void Tide techniques were only effective against one sense at any given time. No matter how quickly you managed to deactivate the others, there would inevitably be a time lag tipping the target off.

And so, after much deliberation, Eishirou had struck upon a solution—a Void Tide technique that worked slowly. As a matter of course, Void Tide techniques relied on biological reflexes to produce immediate results. However, if those effects could be delayed, it wouldn't be impossible to use several of them simultaneously. In effect, it would block out all five senses—sight, hearing, smell, taste, and touch—and leave the target in a state of utter defenselessness.

The greatest advantage of Void Tide techniques was that the target tended to remain unaware of how they had been affected. And so Eishirou had been busy applying them to Baldanders since the moment he realized escape was impossible.

However, their precise application had been remarkably difficult—a race against time to see whether his foe's trap would close first, or whether he could buy enough time to fully cut off Baldanders's senses.

In the end, Eishirou had won by a hairbreadth.

"Ha-ha...! You got me... I hate to say it... But you're pretty good, huh...?"

With those final words, Baldanders swayed unsteadily before falling headfirst in a heap.

Just as the dull sound of the impact echoed out, the threads holding Eishirou in place dissipated.

Spinning through the air, he alighted in an empty lot. The building, it seemed, really had been decomposed. Once again, the thought of that horrifying Orga Lux shook him to his core.

He kept his distance from his fallen adversary just to be sure, but his foe didn't seem to be breathing. Eishirou listened carefully to make sure that his heart had likewise stopped beating.

He was dead, all right.

"...All right! I won!" he exclaimed, making a little victory pose.

Against, of all foes, Odd Eye.

The most powerful intelligence operative in the world.

Despite everything, Eishirou had—

"...Hey, now. Are you sure about that?"

"Huh...?"

Before his very eyes, Baldanders's lifeless body rose slowly to its feet.

*

"What...?! Wh-what...?!" Eishirou mouthed as he backed slowly away.

Baldanders—or rather, Melchior—scratched the back of his head. "Geez. It's been a while since I last died. There's just no getting used to it."

He lifted a hand to his throat, but the wound had already vanished.

Indeed, his neck, which had broken when he had fallen to the ground, was likewise completely healed.

"A regenerative...? No, that can't be... How is it that even possible? Not even the best regenerative can resuscitate themselves..."

Eishirou was visibly confused but still ready for further combat, revealing not even the faintest opening. He was, at the end of the day, an excellent agent, to the extent that Melchior would have liked to have recruited him for Grimalkin.

Hmm...? Hold on, didn't the last Odd Eye say something about trying to recruit a kid from the Yabuki clan...?

It was impossible to know whether he had meant the boy presently before him, but if so, Melchior's predecessor had certainly had a good eye.

Now that he had confronted him out in the field like this, however, there was no way he could allow him to escape.

"Well, I'll let you have the first win. But you aren't getting any more," Melchior said.

Eishirou, still on guard, took another half step backward. "Um, before that... How are you still alive? You were dead, right? Like, completely."

"I'll let you keep guessing."

Melchior was willing to talk so long as was necessary, but there was no point revealing his hand.

The Orga Lux embedded in his heart—No Name—was his most vital secret. Even at Le Wolfe Black Institute, the only other person who knew of its existence was Dirk himself.

Even the appellation "No Name" was a pseudonym.

An Orga Lux like his, which granted its user pseudo-immortality, wasn't even supposed to exist. When Solnage had uncovered the characteristics of its urm-manadite, its executives had elected without hesitation to keep it top secret. That decision, no doubt, had been reached on account of the vicious cost demanded by the Orga Lux (and just personally, Melchior suspected the other foundations had at least a few Orga Luxes they kept confidential for similar reasons).

The cost that his exacted was *life*.

No Name maintained its stock by consuming human lives. So long as its stock was not depleted, it could revive its user—several times over, if necessary. The problem was that it needed to consume a life every two months. In other words, six people would have to be sacrificed each year for someone to keep using it. If two months passed without adding to its stock, it would take the user's life instead.

At present, No Name had nine lives in its reserve—although as Melchior had just consumed one of them, it was technically down to eight.

As the user was forced into a comatose state whenever No Name fed, not even he knew how the Orga Lux did it. Nor did he know or even care how Solnage chose and prepared those who would be fed to it next. As far as he was concerned, the only thing that mattered was prolonging his own life.

And there was another important by-product of No Name's abilities.

He could use as many other Orga Luxes as he had lives in No Name's stock. If a new user was found, they would naturally take priority—but otherwise, Melchior was free to borrow any Orga Luxes in Le Wolfe's possession that were presently without users.

"I underestimated you a little. I guess I owe you an apology," he said to the Yabuki kid.

"Not at all. By all means, keep on underestimating me," Eishirou responded with a twitchy smile.

"I'll have to be a little more careful this time. A little more cowardly."

Unfortunately, the Orga Lux corresponding to the life that had been consumed was Arachne's Thread, and he was now unable to wield it. At least he still had the others on hand.

"Well then, let's get on with the second round."

Just as he was about to retrieve his next Lux—

"…!"

Every sign of Dirk's presence was snuffed out.

A quick glance over his shoulder revealed that the vehicle he had come in was gone, vanished, leaving behind only the Grimalkin bodyguard in a clear state of confusion.

"Oh…?"

Eishirou too, after a moment's delay, picked up on this development, following his gaze.

At first, Melchior had taken this for another of the Yabuki kid's tricks, but he quickly reconsidered that thought.

The car hadn't driven away—it had simply vanished. No doubt it was the work of another of Le Wolfe's Orga Luxes, Atlas's Perone, which allowed its user to teleport objects between set coordinates fixed in advance. One of those coordinates, Melchior knew, was set to the site of the Festa.

Its current user, if he wasn't mistaken, was one of Dirk's protégés.

Which means this was his plan from the very beginning...

Ostensibly, this operation was about Dirk putting himself out as bait to fish for agents from Galaxy so Melchior could eliminate them—but had his actual goal been to use this kid as an excuse to lure Melchior himself away so he could up and vanish?

Tch...! I've been played...

Grimalkin was Le Wolfe's intelligence organization, and while it was officially under the command of the student council president, it was in reality strongly influenced by Solnage. For some time now, Melchior had been conducting surveillance of Dirk's security entourage on Solnage's orders. For reasons unknown to him, Dirk had apparently been acting in a manner that headquarters found worthy of suspicion.

"Oh dear. Your boss seems to have up and vanished all of a sudden... Is everything okay?"

Melchior hadn't intended to let his annoyance show, but while Eishirou couldn't have possibly known everything that was going on, he did seem particularly sensitive to these kinds of subtleties.

"Hey, don't mind me," he continued. "If you want to chase after him, be my guest. I don't think I'd be able to escape with you on my tail anyway."

"..."

"Well, I don't know how long I'll be able to keep up, but I'll do my best to fight back. Let's get started, then," Eishirou said blithely, readying a kunai knife.

If he was to cross blades with this boy again, Melchior knew he wouldn't lose a second time. He had been caught off guard earlier, and while Eishirou's Void Tide techniques were a threat, they would hardly prevail against his full strength.

But…whether the fight could be settled quickly was another matter.

Eishirou had basically declared that he was willing to fight him in an effort to buy time. If he resisted with all his skills and abilities, it would take Melchior a good while to fell him, no matter how many Orga Luxes he used.

The effective range of Atlas's Perone is about a hundred meters… And given its current specs, it'll be limited to around three uses. There's still a chance I can track him down…

"Ah… I guess I've got no choice," he said. "We'll just have to postpone this showdown until next time."

Melchior hated the idea of letting go of someone who knew about his abilities, even if only partially, but his priority right now had to be tracking down Dirk's whereabouts.

"Personally, I'd rather not fight with you ever again, if I can help it," Eishirou answered.

"…You've got gall, kid. Fine. I'm going."

Sparing a sidelong glance at Eishirou's grinning face, Melchior called out to Dirk's abandoned bodyguard and leaped out from the empty lot.

*

Once Baldanders was gone, Eishirou stared after him for a moment into the darkness. Finally, deciding that it was probably safe for him to leave, he let out a deep sigh.

"Ah, that was close…!"

If Baldanders had set his sights on taking Eishirou's life, he would have been killed for sure. Neither his Void Tide techniques nor his Fivefold Seal were easily defeated, but they weren't invulnerable, either. There was little doubt that a foe as skilled as Baldanders would have found a way to break past them.

In any case, Eishirou had to admit he had made a narrow escape.

At that moment, his mobile began to ring with an incoming call. It was voice-only, the number withheld.

Then again, very few individuals had his number in the first place. "Yeah, yeah, I'm here. Who's this?"

"Oh, so you're still kicking? Impressive."

Sure enough, the voice on the other end of the line belonged to the boss of the man who had just been gunning for his life.

"You used me as bait, you son of a bitch."

"So what? It's your fault for being such a pest in the first place," Dirk spat back in his usual irritated tone of voice. *"But that Melchior guy was just as much of a pain in the ass as you. Good job beating him."*

"If you're talking about Baldanders, he looked pretty damn bloodthirsty when he took off after you. You sure you should be taking it so easy?"

"There's no problem. Now that I'm away, he won't find me." Dirk paused there for a moment before continuing, *"So I guess I owe you my gratitude. Thanks for the help."*

"Hah? *Thanks?"* Eishirou's eyes bulged. He never would have expected to hear such a thing from the Tyrant of all people.

"So I'm gonna clue you in to what they're looking for."

"...How do I know I can believe you?"

"Believe me or don't, that's up to you. But it's your job to weigh up the intel, right?"

Indeed, it certainly was Eishirou's responsibility to consider all the evidence.

Then again...he could hardly think of a less trustworthy source.

Of course, if Dirk was being truthful here, it would be a major breakthrough. And for all his faults, he wasn't dishonest. After all, he understood that those who lied in his business didn't last long—not for moral reasons, but as a matter of simple profit and loss.

In this case, however, Dirk was calling him of his own accord. There was no deal being done here, and it would be Eishirou's own fault if he let himself get taken advantage of. There was no logical reason why Dirk should give him any intel.

In that case, it was sensible to suspect a trap…

"…Well, I guess I'll hear you out, then."

"*Hmph. Just shut up and listen. See, the people you're looking for— you'll find them above and below.*"

CHAPTER 4
A RAY OF LIGHT

It was early morning, and Claudia had gathered everyone in a room in Hotel Elnath for an emergency meeting.

"It's definitely a trap, right?"

"I—I think so, too…"

Sylvia and Kirin were both immediately suspicious when they heard the information Eishirou had just brought back. Saya, currently in a coma due to the toxins from her match against Orphelia, would no doubt have had a similar reaction if she were present.

Eishirou, probably exhausted, had collapsed after his return.

"It's crazy to trust the Tyrant of all people. I know we don't have anything else to work from at the moment, but this is *worse* than clutching at straws," Sylvia said with a wave of her hand, heaving a sigh.

"Besides…," Kirin added, "what does that even mean, they're *above and below*? It's too vague to really tell us anything…"

"You're both right, of course," Claudia noted. "However, given the lengths Eishirou had to go to for this information, it would be a shame to discard it without first weighing it up."

At that moment, Ayato raised his hand. "Do you have anything that could add credence to it?" he asked.

Claudia was a compassionate person, but not one to let herself be swayed by emotion. No matter how difficult it had been for Eishirou to obtain this information, if its credibility was low, she wouldn't have thought it worth discussing.

"I don't have specific proof, if that's what you mean… But before we get to that, what do *you* think, Ayato?"

"Me…? Yeah, I have my doubts. But then again, if they did want to lure us into a trap, wouldn't it make sense to give us a more specific location? Like Kirin said, it's too vague."

"Maybe they're just trying to confuse us?" Sylvia remarked, her skepticism undeterred.

Well, one could hardly blame her for thinking that way.

Ayato too had met Dirk Eberwein in person, and he hadn't exactly come across as trustworthy.

"About that… By *below*, there's at least one place that comes to mind," Claudia said.

"The underground block, you mean?" Ayato asked.

"Exactly." Claudia flashed him a soft smile.

"I understand that much, but the underground block is huge," Sylvia added. "It would take forever to search through it properly. And besides, wouldn't Stjarnagarm have noticed something during their regular patrols? …Right, Helga?"

Having stayed silent up until now, the commander of the city guard, Helga Lindwall, wore an unusually apologetic look. "I'm sorry, but I'm afraid I'm not particularly proud of the current situation on that front…"

"Huh…?"

Ayato, Kirin, and Sylvia each exchanged worried looks.

"What do you mean?"

Haruka, who had been waiting quietly by Helga's side, spoke up.

"Well, you see… Ha-ha, this is a bit of a pickle…," she said evasively.

After removing the shard of the Raksha-Nada with the help of Elliot Forster and his Lei-Glems several days prior, Haruka had thrown herself into her duties as a member of Stjarnagarm with more vigor than ever before. She seemed perfectly at home in her uniform now.

"I was going to wait until after we cleared up the other issue, but seeing as the one connects to the other, perhaps we should deliver our report now...? Do you mind?" Helga asked.

"Please, go ahead." Claudia nodded.

For her part, Claudia seemed already familiar with the particulars.

No doubt she had likewise consulted with her mother Isabella, who couldn't make it to this meeting as she was currently attending the Concordia.

"As a matter of fact, an informant approached me earlier today... or yesterday, given the hour..."

"An informant?"

"Ernesta Kühne of Allekant Académie."

"...!" Kirin caught her breath. "About the autonomous puppets, you mean?"

"Precisely."

The puppets that Kirin had encountered in the lakeside city— clearly under the control of the Golden Bough Alliance—apparently resembled Ardy in appearance and abilities.

"She summed it up like this: It seems that a large number of puppets she designed for a previous contract have been brought into Asterisk, and she's concerned that they're being used illegitimately. She doesn't want the authorities to think she's involved with the culprits, so she wanted to provide us with information to prove her innocence, should anything happen."

"That all sounds...rather convenient. But I'm sure she managed to keep up a look of nonchalance as she told you this," Claudia said, pressing her hand against her cheek as she forced a smile.

Judging from her reaction, Claudia must have already received a report on the matter, even if she didn't know all the details.

"That sounds more like she's looking to make a deal than give information," Sylvia said, pulling a face. "Isn't she basically asking to be let go in exchange for her cooperation?"

"Even so, we're desperate for whatever information we can get our hands on. I can't deny it feels like we're being taken advantage of, but I don't think Ernesta Kühne was actually involved in the Golden Bough Alliance. It seems she doesn't even know their true objective."

"...Really?" Sylvia asked, still dubious.

"One of our Stregas at Stjarnagarm is capable of seeing through lies and deception," Haruka added. "It only works on someone willing to be read, and it can't be used for evidence, but we were able to confirm that she was telling the truth."

"Huh. I didn't know that."

"Well, it isn't something we make public. Anyway, according to Ernesta Kühne, the Golden Bough Alliance is composed of three members: Lamina Mortis, Dirk Eberwein, and the Varda-Vaos."

"What about Erenshkigal and Agrestia?"

"Ernesta tells us that only those three are involved in the decision-making. Everyone else is just a tool to be used."

"If I remember right, it was Ecknardt, Lamina Mortis, and the Varda-Vaos who put together the last plan...," Haruka said, putting her finger to her temple as she rummaged through her memories. "Right. So Dirk Eberwein must be new, to take over Ecknardt's role."

"That brings us to the main issue. The most valuable information Ernesta gave us is about the puppets that have been brought into Asterisk. She provided us with their number and location, as well as their specifications."

Kirin raised a timid hand. "U-um... The captain did say they were produced en masse...but is it really possible to make so many of them? Those puppets—*Valiants*, Percival called them—they're powerful weapons. Probably only ranked Genestella would be able to stand up to them in a one-on-one fight. And against more than one, maybe only Page Ones would be able to resist. If they're brought in by the dozen..."

"By the thousand."

"What...?"

"Ernesta Kühne claims to have delivered a thousand units to her client."

The room suddenly turned tense.

Ayato and Sylvia hadn't faced the puppets directly, but given what Kirin had told them, it sounded like they would prove a major headache.

And there were a *thousand* of them?

"Wait a minute. How did Ernesta know they've been brought here? And their locations, too...?"

"She seems to have installed some extra functions to let her, and only her, track them—security in case something goes wrong."

"That's either very forward thinking of her, or else..."

Ernesta's seemingly innocent and cheerful smile hid the depths of her strength and resolve well.

"Anyway, we used that information to raid a warehouse, where we found twenty of those things."

"Ah."

"...Everything was going smoothly at first... But the Valiants activated when I got there, and I had no choice but to destroy them."

"...Oh."

It was hard to tell whether that served as proof the information was accurate or if it only underscored the possibility it had all been a trap.

"Huh...? Um, are you saying...you went there alone, commander...?"

"We're short on manpower. Most of my subordinates, Haruka included, had to be assigned to monitoring the perimeter and redirecting the public to a safe distance. Besides, we hadn't yet seen what those Valiants are capable of firsthand, and I didn't want to place my people in harm's way unnecessarily."

Still, given that Kirin had just opined that even a Page One would have a hard time going up against them, to think that Helga seemed to have defeated twenty all by herself...

"I rushed to the scene when I heard the noise. But by the time I got there, it was already over...," Haruka added with an awkward smile.

"The problem is what happened next. Once the Valiants activated, the live tracking data that Ernesta provided us was lost."

"Huh?"

"Of course, we still have the data backups, which we've used to continue our search...but the puppets seem to have been relocated."

"So you're saying the Golden Bough Alliance anticipated all this?" Claudia asked, spreading her hands wide in a show of exasperation. She was left with no choice but to laugh.

"I would say they deliberately overlooked the tracking mechanism that Ernesta Kühne installed in the Valiants and turned the situation to their own advantage. From our perspective at Stjarnagarm, having confirmed the presence of one batch of units, we're left with no choice but to search all the other locations, too."

"Indeed. We've already had to dedicate a considerable portion of our people to security at the Concordia, and there's more trouble than usual among the tourists this year, too. Add to that a large-scale investigation of multiple warehouses and storage facilities, and we're stretched to our limit." Averting her gaze, Helga took a deep breath before adding, "And the biggest problem is that the warehouse we found the Valiants in was already included in the patrol routes I recently set up for this case."

"...What does that mean?" Sylvia asked, eyes narrowed.

"When I questioned the officer responsible, he told me he knew it was part of his established route, but in light of the security situation, he prioritized areas more likely to see disturbances. In other words, he looked the other way."

"Th-that...certainly is a problem."

"My thoughts exactly. To his credit, he's an honest officer, not one to shirk his duties. He's never done anything to warrant a disciplinary punishment. After the interrogation, he couldn't understand why he had even done it."

"You know what they say, Stjarnagarm is short-staffed because Commander Helga is so demanding during the selection process," Haruka followed up. "I'm just a newbie at this point."

Helga's expression, however, remained stern. "Given the situation, I asked Director Korbel to put the officer in question under psycho-sensory examination as soon as possible. The hospital's tests take time, but they're more accurate than those regularly conducted on IEF executives. As I feared, the director detected traces of mental interference—brainwashing—albeit in very small quantities."

"So it *was* the Varda-Vaos…!"

"In all likelihood. No doubt the effect was fueled by my people's zeal to maintain security and prioritize immediate disturbances… But getting back to the point at hand, there's no way to know that something similar wouldn't happen with any large-scale investigation of the underground block."

"…!"

So that was how it all connected? In that case, there was definitely a possibility that the Golden Bough Alliance was lying low in the underground block.

"Above all, the most important lesson to take to heart from all this is just how brutal the Varda-Vaos's abilities are. Typically, one's prana will resist any mental suggestions that run contrary to their own will—however, there are clearly work-arounds. If the victim believes they're acting according to their own beliefs, they can be manipulated into furthering the aims of the enemy… There may be more people than we can imagine who have been influenced that way."

"…"

That was a scary thought.

To think you could be involved in their plot without even realizing it. Perhaps not even Ayato or the others were immune.

"…"

A heavy silence fell over the room, broken only when Claudia's mobile began to ring with an incoming call.

"My apologies... Yes... Is that so...? I understand... We'll be there shortly..."

After a brief conversation, Claudia glanced up at everyone and announced, "Saya has woken up. She has something important to tell us all, so she wants us to see her at once."

At those words, everyone present stood up.

Saya seemed to have had some success talking with Orphelia during her semifinal match. Perhaps she had managed to garner some valuable information.

"My apologies. We'll have to return to headquarters soon... I wish I could send Haruka to join you, but unfortunately I can't spare her right now," Helga said with a rueful shake of her head.

"I'm sorry, everyone... Of course, I'll keep looking into the Golden Bough Alliance as best I can," Haruka added, clasping her hands together in front her face with an apologetic bow.

It was she who had the strongest connection with the Golden Bough Alliance, so it was natural that she wanted to be at the forefront of this investigation.

But at the same time, it was equally clear that Stjarnagarm was undermanned, so she wouldn't be able to abandon her official duties, either.

"Not at all," Claudia said. "The first obligation of the city guard is to maintain peace and security throughout Asterisk. Please focus your attentions on that."

"...We're counting on you," Ayato added.

"Ah, say hi to Saya for me, Ayato," Haruka said. "Let her know I'm glad she's okay."

Helga gave Claudia a brief nod, and then she and Haruka hurried from the room.

"Dawn is breaking, even if the sun isn't up yet...," Kirin murmured as she turned her gaze out the window after seeing them off.

Indeed, thick, ominous clouds hung low over the midwinter sky.

*

"...You took forever!"

No sooner did they all enter her hospital room than Saya, waiting there with her arms crossed, puffed her cheeks out. She wasn't wearing a hospital gown as might be expected, but rather her usual school uniform, and she didn't particularly look like someone who had been in a coma until just a short while ago.

"S-Saya...? Are you sure you should be up and about?" Ayato asked.

"I'm okay. I got my arm looked at by a healer, and there's nothing else wrong with me," she answered, flexing her muscles for everyone to see.

That was good news, but the fact that she had been seen to by a healer at all meant that she must have sustained serious injuries, the kind that would leave long-term effects if treated through ordinary means. It was clearer than ever how reckless it had been for her to participate in that last match despite her weakened state.

"Th-thank goodness...! It looks like the toxins have been cleared, too!" Kirin exclaimed, sighing with relief.

"Yep. I'm a hundred percent back to normal," Saya answered, flashing her a victory sign.

She certainly did look like her usual self.

"That's what matters most. Now then...what's this urgent matter you wanted to tell us?" Claudia asked, a sense of danger lurking behind her smile.

"Shhh!" Saya lifted a finger to her lips, glancing around worriedly.

Of course, they were in a private room, so there was no one else around.

"...Isn't Isabella coming?"

"My mother? Ah, she's preoccupied at the moment. I haven't seen her face-to-face yet, either. I believe she's still on the ferry."

"Oh. Good."

"What's wrong with Claudia's mom joining us?" Sylvia asked.

Saya looked unsettled. "You'll understand once I fill you in."

And so, she recounted what she had heard from Orphelia during their match.

It wasn't a long account, but the faces of everyone gathered soon turned bleak.

"So that's everything I heard from Erenshkigal."

By the time she finished telling them the shocking news, no one could even bring themselves to respond.

Orphelia's ultimate goal was to eliminate everyone in Asterisk.

They didn't know her reasoning, but there was no doubt she had the power to pull it off.

And they had virtually no way of stopping her.

The first person to speak up was Kirin. "W-we have to do something…! Anything…! Somehow, whatever the cost, we have to stop her…!" Her lips were trembling, her fists clenched tightly as her face turned deathly pale.

Next was Sylvia, outwardly calm, but wearing the most severe expression Ayato had ever seen on her face. "Yes. I agree with you a hundred percent… But how…? What do you think, Claudia?"

"…From what we've just heard, it will be difficult if the Golden Bough Alliance has already completed its preparations," Claudia stated calmly, though her bright voice seemed slightly strained. "In other words, they could flip the switch at any moment. The second we make an attempt to stop either the bomb—Orphelia Landlufen herself—or the ringleaders Lamina Mortis and Dirk Eberwein, they'll immediately set it off. And with the group's level of influence within the foundations, it will be impossible to move against them in secret."

Though she had likely anticipated a great many possibilities regarding the Golden Bough Alliance's true purpose, no doubt she had still been taken by surprise.

"But I understand why you didn't want my mother to hear of this, Saya."

"Huh? What do you mean?" Kirin asked.

Saya was the one who offered up a response: "Isabella—or Galaxy, I suppose—would choose a strategy based on sacrifice. I couldn't stand that."

"A strategy based on sacrifice...?"

"To use the previous analogy, think of this as a bomb about to explode," Claudia said. "She'll be thinking about how to reduce the damage to Galaxy, how to conceal the existence of the Varda-Vaos after the explosion, and if possible, how to connect the Golden Bough Alliance to one of the other foundations instead. That sort of thing..." Claudia paused there, letting out a bitter sigh. "If it can't be stopped, that *would* seem the logical course of action."

"I guess, as things stand, there's only one way to stop this," Saya observed. "If, during her match against Orphelia Landlufen, Julis could—"

"No," Ayato interrupted sternly. "She'll never do that. Never."

"I know. I wouldn't want that for her, either." Saya nodded in agreement.

"Then we'll have to think of some other way... Hmm..." Sylvia crossed her arms as she sank into thought.

"Right... Didn't you say it was supposed to be too late by the time you woke up, Saya?"

"Oh, that's because I used up all my prana before the poison could get me."

"...?" Kirin, not understanding, tilted her head to one side.

Claudia, standing beside her, began to explain: "The toxins used on Saya were probably the same ones that affected Ayato while we were in Lieseltania. It seems that the length of the coma depends on the total amount of one's prana, so if you exhaust your prana before the poison can take effect, it makes sense that you would wake up faster as a result."

"Ah, so *that* was the point of your final shot with the Helnekraum." Ayato nodded.

Saya had done well to come up with that idea on the spur of the moment.

"Exactly."

"You've given us time to prepare countermeasures, so well done, Saya," Claudia concluded.

"Hee-hee." Saya puffed out her chest with pride.

"...Time...? Time...?" Kirin suddenly looked up. "Ah, um, I...I just had an idea..."

"Huh...?!"

Everyone suddenly turned toward her.

"U-um, just wait a minute! I don't know if it will actually work, and there's at least one condition—no, two—that need to be cleared first...!"

"That can wait...! Just tell us what you're thinking!" Claudia demanded, drawing closer to her.

Taking one more look at everyone's faces, Kirin nervously revealed her thoughts.

"..."

Once they had heard her out, they all sank into thought.

"I see... Then there *is* a possibility," Claudia finally murmured.

Certainly, they couldn't expect to solve all their problems this way, and it would, of course, be a very fine needle to thread, but given the circumstances...

"Like Kirin said, the hard part will be setting up the preconditions," Saya noted. "At the very least, we'll need to know the whereabouts of Madiath Mesa, Dirk Eberwein, and the Varda-Vaos..."

"Back to square one, then...hmm...," Sylvia grumbled.

"About that... Sylvia, can't you find them using that song of yours?"

"Huh? To some extent, I guess... But you know I won't be able to narrow down the exact location, right?"

Seeing as Stjarnagarm, which no doubt had individuals with expert detection abilities within its ranks, hadn't been able to locate them, it stood to reason that the members of the Golden Bough Alliance had taken fairly solid measures to conceal their locations.

"I've heard the accuracy of detection abilities can be increased by narrowing down the range, so if we can pinpoint a certain area, wouldn't it be possible to sense some kind of reaction even if they have taken precautions?"

"That's... I've never tried it, so I'm not sure... Maybe?" Sylvia tilted her head to one side, deep in thought. "Still, how would we know where to focus?"

"I can answer that." Claudia pulled out her mobile and activated a three-dimensional projection of Asterisk. "We should start here...," she said, pointing to the ballast area in the underground block on the map—the area closest to the main stage being used for the Festa. "Lamina Mortis—Madiath Mesa—is probably around here."

"...!"

Everyone jolted in surprise, but Sylvia quickly regained her composure and took a deep breath. Then, softly—

"Thought and memory, thou winged twins, fly, o swiftly fly, and tell me the lair of lurking demons."

The lyrics were a little different, but it was similar to the song she had used when looking for Flora during her kidnapping.

She must have been using considerable prana, as mana raged throughout the room.

At that moment, two black feathers appeared on the three-dimensional map.

"Beyond the clouds of dawn, upon the winds of twilight, from the edge of nightfall, lead us onward..."

When they had been searching for Flora, the two feathers had roved all across the map, but this time, they didn't move from the spot where the Festa stage was located, simply spinning around and around.

"Black emissaries, thought and memory, fly down to me and reveal now thy truth..."

As she sang, a tiny glimmer of light lit up beneath the wings, then quickly disappeared.

"Phew..." Wiping the sweat from her forehead, she let out a heavy sigh. "It was a small reaction, very subtle, but I felt it. Lamina Mortis really is down there."

"...!"

Apart from Claudia, the rest of the room stared back in astonishment.

"...But how did you know?"

"I just trusted what the Tyrant said. 'Above and below.' By *below*, I assumed he meant somewhere in the underground block. From what we've heard from Haruka and Ayato, Madiath Mesa sounds like quite the sentimental type. At the very least, he certainly has a strong attachment to the past. So it stands to reason that he would be lurking somewhere with a close connection to his own history."

"But I thought it wasn't possible to receive or send communications from the underground block," Saya remarked, remembering how she had gotten lost down there once before.

After all, wouldn't it be incredibly inconvenient for his plans if he couldn't contact the outside world?

"General communications aren't available down there," Claudia responded without hesitation. "But I'm sure that can be fixed by going through the management department with jurisdiction over the underground facility. That would probably be trivial for the Golden Bough Alliance."

"I see..."

With that, everyone in the room was convinced.

But that wasn't the end of it.

"I know you must be tired, but in that case, Sylvia, could you search *above* this time?"

"What...?! Do you know where to look there, too?"

"It's only conjecture. But the Varda-Vaos *must* be up there. I was stunned myself when I realized the possibility...but I'm now all but convinced," Claudia said, pointing out the window to—

"Hotel Elnath...?"

"...The top floor?"

In other words, the very hotel where Ayato and the others had convened just a short while before.

"Ahhhhh! Right, I see what you mean...!" Sylvia held her head in her hands, seemingly chastising herself for not realizing it sooner. "The site of the Rikka Garden Summit, right?"

The Rikka Garden Summit: a famous dome-shaped aerial garden on the top floor of Hotel Elnath, where the student council presidents of Asterisk's six schools met formally once a month—and which was otherwise off-limits to all, even executives of the IEFs.

Sure enough, when Sylvia used her ability once more, she felt a similar reaction.

"Ah... I was careless," she said. "The garden is maintained almost entirely by autonomous puppets, and on top of that, it's used only once a month. There's no better place to hide..."

"This is only a guess, but the Varda-Vaos may have been based there this whole time," Claudia observed.

"You've got to be kidding... So we've been having our monthly meetings in the enemy's lair this whole time?"

"We've also been holding our meetings to resist them right at the enemy's doorstep."

Indeed, people tended to overlook what was near at hand, but this seemed ridiculous.

"This is as far as I can go, though," Claudia said with a shrug. "I'm afraid I don't know where the Tyrant is. Since he offered up this information himself, it's probably fair to say he's not with the others."

"It's good enough though, right?" Sylvia said. "But you seem to have taken the Tyrant at his word right from the beginning. Why?"

"It's simple. I don't trust him as a person, but I trust his character," Claudia answered with a meaningful smile.

"The Tyrant's *character*...?"

"Well, I've known him a little longer than you all have. I have a good grasp of him, I think. He's more obsessed with frustrating winners than with seizing victory himself." Claudia paused there, clapping her hands to change the subject. "Now, I'm afraid I don't have any idea where he might be, so we'll just have to try to locate him through other means... I'm thinking we should leave that task to Yabuki."

"By himself? But isn't that a little much for one person...?"

Wasn't what happened last night proof enough of just how much danger would be involved?

"This operation will only prove successful if it's carried out by people we know we can trust. If the only thing that mattered here was fighting potential, we could, of course, seek reinforcements from my mother. But that would be meaningless in this case."

"Putting aside whether to trust Yabuki, Claudia is right," Saya added. "Given the Varda-Vaos's abilities, we need to keep the number of people involved to a minimum."

"Well, I guess you're right. Besides, our job is going to be even more dangerous, isn't it?" Despite her words, Sylvia's face was brimming with determination.

It was little wonder. She had been searching for someone precious to her for years, and now she had a chance to finally reach her.

"Hmm... All right. Let's leave it to Eishirou."

Ayato felt a little guilty, but this was a critical juncture, after all.

They couldn't afford to waste any more time.

"Which brings us to that other *condition*, so to speak."

"Y-yes...! If we go with this strategy, we're going to need Julis's help...," Kirin added in a small voice, glancing up at Ayato.

"All right. I'll have a talk with her."

Checking the time, he realized it was now past nine o'clock.

The championship match was scheduled for noon, so there was little time left.

"Very well," Claudia said. "We'll proceed with the other preparations, and we'll leave Julis to you, Ayato."

CHAPTER 5
REMINISCENCES

"Phew…"

Julis let the warm water from the shower wash over her as she shook off her drowsiness.

No doubt due to her exhaustion, she had fallen asleep last night without meaning to. She still had some time before the championship match, but she was supposed to have already entered the venue by now to start her warm-ups.

And yet…

"I wasn't expecting my prana to have recovered this much… Is it because of that potion the Ban'yuu Tenra gave me?"

Her *Queen of the Night* ability drained her reserves of prana to their limit. Under normal circumstances, one night's rest wouldn't have been enough to replenish them.

Xinglou had said it was just for peace of mind, but it seemed to be considerably more effective than that.

Or else…

Every time I use the Queen of the Night, *it feels like there's something strange growing inside me…*

It still wasn't clear whether that was good or bad.

Either way, it didn't matter anymore.

Because today, she was going to settle everything, once and for all.

"I'm not in perfect condition, but at least I'm back to around eighty percent. Hopefully, that will be good enough..."

Though the fracture in her right arm was difficult to work around, it was expected that just about any fighter would have sustained some manner of injury by the time they reached the championship. Not even Orphelia, with all her overwhelming power, could get to that level completely unharmed.

With that thought, Julis stepped out from the bathroom, wiped her body down with a towel, and stared at her face in the mirror.

...She didn't look too bad. A little nervous, sure, but not distracted or intimidated. Maybe that was because she had been able to unload one of her burdens from the past year in the previous day's semifinal match.

Anyway, so long as she wasn't suffering from any physical or mental maladies, all she had to do was keep pressing on.

After putting on her underwear, she slapped herself on the sides of her face a few times to fire herself up. Just then—

"Hmm...?"

She heard a noise from the living room and immediately gave it her full attention.

There was clearly someone in there.

One of Orphelia's people, maybe...?

She reached out for her Rect Lux—only to realize that she didn't have it on hand. That being the case, she concentrated as much of her prana as possible, readied herself to deploy her abilities at the earliest possible warning, and leaped out from the bathroom.

"Who's there?!"

"Whoa...?!"

What she found was a familiar face, his eyes opening wide in shock and alarm.

The young man's body, garbed in the uniform of Seidoukan Academy, stood motionless, as though he had just turned to stone.

"Huh? Ayato...? You surprised me."

One look at his face was enough to calm her nerves as she brought a hand to her breast.

She likewise relaxed her prana, and the mana swirling around them soon dissipated.

"I—I'm sorry...!"

Ayato, on the other hand, spun quickly around, his face having turned bright red.

Only then did Julis finally realize she was dressed in nothing more than her underwear—and with that, she too felt the blood rushing to her face, all the way to the tips of her ears.

"...! A-Ayato...! H-how dare you...?!"

She rushed to collect her uniform from her bed and did her best to muster her voice into a roar...only to realize that she wasn't truly upset over this situation.

On the contrary, it prompted a sense of déjà vu...

"...Bah! Ha-ha...!"

"J-Julis?"

As she burst into laughter, Ayato's confused voice sounded behind her.

"Oh, it's just... This reminded me of how we first met."

Right...

Looking back on it, it wasn't the worst possible first meeting.

But to think it was happening all over again...

"It just brought back memories. It's almost funny, even... Wait a minute; let me get changed." As she spoke, she quickly put her arms through the sleeves of her uniform.

"Sorry, Julis. There's something urgent I need to discuss with you... I tried calling you a few times."

Why was he apologizing over and over like this?

Checking her mobile as she put on her clothes, she saw that he had indeed called her several times. She hadn't noticed, since she had rushed to take a shower right after waking up.

"I know you didn't mean to catch me unawares like that. I mean, we've known each other for ages now, right?"

"...Right." Responding after a short pause, Ayato's voice had a nostalgic ring to it.

That alone was enough to bring her a glimmer of joy.

"All right then, fire away," Julis said after she finished dressing.

Ayato, still slightly nervous, turned back around.

"So? What did you want to talk about? Don't tell me you've come all this way just to give me a handkerchief?"

If it was urgent, it had to be important.

"...There's something I need to ask you. About today's match."

"Yeah, I guessed as much, given the timing." Julis breathed a short sigh, then sat down on the edge of her bed and folded her legs. "But I'm afraid if it's about that, I don't plan on listening—"

"I know. About everything."

Julis looked up with a start.

"I know about the burden you're carrying... Saya straight-up asked Erenshkigal during her own match and then told the rest of us."

"...!"

Julis found herself temporarily lost for words, but she soon regained her composure.

Xinglou had certainly mentioned that Saya and Orphelia seemed to be having some sort of conversation during their semifinal match. She hadn't been able to discern the actual contents of their discussion, but to think Orphelia had fully divulged the truth to her... If she really wanted to see that plan of hers come to fruition, there would have been no need for her to do that. But at the same time, if she wanted to bring an end to it, there ought to have been other options available to her, as well.

...*No, stop it. I can confront her about that myself. More importantly...*

"I see. So you know the truth now?"

As far as Julis was concerned, that wasn't happy news.

There was nothing to be gained from knowing about one's

inevitable doom. All that knowledge would do was inflict frustration and despair. In that case, the others would be happier not knowing anything at all.

"Don't worry. Like I said yesterday, I'll stop Orphelia. You have my word. If I can't, then, then…!"

She clenched her fists tightly.

She couldn't let her determination falter.

"It's okay, Julis. We can stop their plot. That's why I came here."

"What? But how…?"

While she didn't know the details, she had heard that the people behind Orphelia had spread their tentacles far and wide. They had eyes and ears everywhere, and they would order Orphelia to immediately put their plan into effect if they detected even the slightest sign of interference.

Of course, it was possible that Orphelia herself was bluffing. Julis had considered that possibility more times than she cared to count. But if it *wasn't* a bluff, if she miscalculated, tens of thousands of lives—no, hundreds of thousands—could be lost. She simply couldn't afford to slip up.

Most importantly, there had been no hint of deception in Orphelia's claim. No matter how much she had changed, Julis still considered her a close friend, one with whom she had shared countless joys and sorrows. She could still tell when she was lying.

"From what Saya learned, Erenshkigal is basically just a tool as far the people behind her are concerned—according to her own words, a '*tool of fate*,'" Ayato added. "She might not be ready to refuse them, but she's certainly not acting according to her own free will. Right?"

"…Yeah, it seems that way."

They had only exchanged a few brief conversations, but that certainly was the gist of Orphelia's stance. At the very least, she didn't seem to be actively working to carry out her backers' plan.

"Then we just need to make sure she never gets the order to carry it out."

"Huh…?" Julis's jaw dropped. "Wh-what are you saying…? They can give the order from anywhere, with just a single message…"

Suddenly, she stopped herself, realizing that there might indeed be merit to Ayato's idea.

"Wait… Hold on. Wait. You don't mean…? Are you all…?"

"Yes. The stage is covered with a barrier made from protective gel, one that prevents all communications from getting in and out. So during the match, it doesn't matter what you do."

It was true—there was virtually no way for anyone on the outside to contact someone down on the stage.

Claudia had once taken a wild stab at something similar by breaking into the live commentary studio, but that was about it.

And of course—Julis was sure that they wouldn't anticipate *this*. After all, what was the point preparing for it? As soon as the match was finished, the protective barrier would be lifted and communications restored, so all they had to do was wait. It would be over in a few minutes at best, and a dozen or so at worst.

The only possibility of something going wrong would be if Orphelia died during the course of the match, but unless she was dealt a particularly grievous injury, it would still be possible to revive her with the help of healers standing by outside the arena (as indeed had been the case for Sylvia). Besides, they probably didn't believe there was anyone in Asterisk strong enough to deal her such a blow… Though Julis considered herself capable.

"We've already identified two of the three masterminds. We'll launch our attack at the start of the match to stop them. Yabuki is out looking for the remaining one. So—"

"I get it. Basically, you're asking me to draw it out as long as possible, right?" Julis asked.

Ayato responded with a silent nod.

His strategy required neutralizing those who could give Orphelia her orders while the match was still taking place. If the contest was to end quickly due to an overwhelming attack or something similar, the entire operation would collapse.

"Hmm… It's absurd. I'm surprised Claudia is pushing for it when the odds of success are so slim."

"But they aren't zero, so it's worth a try, right?" Ayato asked, giving her a meaningful look.

"…"

Julis stared back in silence.

There was no need to ask for confirmation. Ayato was always serious.

"…This is ridiculous. You're idiots, the lot of you. You, them, and me as well," she said with a bitter laugh and a deep sigh. "All right. One of the strategies I prepared does involve delaying tactics. I'll put my faith in you all."

If—if it *could* be done, then she wouldn't have to make the worst possible choice.

"Yep. Don't worry. I'll make sure it works out," Ayato said with a weak smile.

The moment she laid eyes on that expression, it felt like a cool wind had just blown through her chest—a gentle breeze blowing away the dark and stagnant dregs that had built up inside her.

"Well, I need to get going then," he said at last.

"…Right. Be careful."

Just as Ayato was about to leave the room through the window, he broke out into a small laugh.

"What's wrong…?"

"No, I just remembered the day we met. Do you remember? *'Now, you die.'* That's what you said to me."

"…Did I?" Julis demurred, but of course she remembered it well.

How could she possibly have forgotten?

It had all started on that day, at that moment.

"If you're feeling nostalgic, I can give you another grand send-off with an Amaryllis attack," Julis said with a chuckle.

"Ha-ha, I think I'm good," Ayato answered with an awkward grin.

Then they each extended an arm, tapping their fists against each other.

"Godspeed, Ayato."

"Yeah. Best of luck to you too, Julis."

With that, Ayato leaped down from the window.

Julis watched after him until he disappeared out of sight—staring after her one and only partner.

*

There was a car parked by the main gate in front of Seidoukan Academy.

When Ayato knocked on the window, the door opened, inviting him inside.

"You look happy. I assume Julis accepted our proposal?" Claudia said.

Alongside her were four others—Saya, Kirin, Eishirou, and Sylvia.

The car, its interior decorated with a table and leather sofas, was similar to the one he had met Dirk in once before. No doubt it was reserved for the student council's exclusive use.

"Yeah. She'll hold up her end."

"Then all that's left is for us to do our best," Sylvia answered.

Ayato, nodding, took a seat by her side.

"Then let's go over our strategy one more time," Claudia began as the car took off.

"We're now heading to the designated starting point, where we'll wait until the agreed time. Just before the championship match gets underway, the protective dome over the stage will be deployed. Ayato, Saya, and Kirin will be responsible for handling Lamina Mortis…or Madiath Mesa. Sylvia and I will go the site of the Rikka Garden Summit where the Varda-Vaos is hiding. Are we in agreement so far?"

"I'm fine with the groups, but…" Ayato glanced toward Saya sitting in front of him. "Does Saya really have to take part in the operation?"

"Of course I do," she responded, unfazed.

"But I mean..."

Her injuries may have been healed, but given that she had been in a coma until just a short while ago, Ayato was reluctant to drag her along with them. He understood that they were shorthanded as it was, that they were about to face an opponent that not even he and Haruka were capable of defeating together...

"I'll be okay. My arms and my prana have recovered. It will be difficult with only the Helnekraum as my main weapon...but it definitely won't slow me down," Saya said with a huff, the look on her face all but announcing she had no intention of backing down.

Ayato knew from experience that there could be no changing her mind when she was as certain as this.

"Hmm... I understand," he answered, raising both hands into the air in surrender.

Claudia, flashing them all a composed smile, continued: "Now, Yabuki, your task is to locate the Tyrant. I've already compiled data on several suspicious locations. You'll be acting alone, and you can begin immediately without waiting for the match to get underway. Even if our opponents catch on to you, it shouldn't be enough to prompt them to initiate their plan immediately. However, if you *are* able to locate him, please wait for the match to begin before acting in any way that might interfere with what he's doing."

"Yeah, yeah, I know. But I'll be honest, I have half a mind to ske-daddle as far from here as I can. I mean, why don't we all get outta here?" Eishirou let out a chuckle to show that he wasn't being serious, but he immediately fell silent when the others fixed him with cold stares.

"We're not asking you to throw your life away, of course," Claudia responded. "If you find yourself in danger, you can do what you like. But until then, keep on doing your job. Do you understand?"

"I know, I know. I'll stick to him until the very last minute...I just wanna check something, though. This data of yours, you got that from calculating back based on the nightmares the Pan-Dora gives you, right?"

"Indeed. The Tyrant and his associates have killed me quite a few times now, so I'm using those experiences to surmise his location and the facilities he's using... What of it?"

"Ah, well, I guess this is a simple question, but you've never seen anything like *this* in your dreams, have you?"

The nightmares that the Pan-Dora forced on Claudia every night were the cost of its usage, showing her again and again the countless ways in which she might die in the future. Given that it posed such an enormous danger, it wouldn't be strange if she had seen Orphelia destroying Asterisk in her dreams.

Nonetheless, she regretfully shook her head. "Nothing at all, I'm afraid. Aside from the Tyrant, neither the Varda-Vaos nor Lamina Mortis has ever appeared in them, either. Of course, I don't always remember everything, so it's possible I simply forgot... But I do have another hypothesis."

"...Another hypothesis?"

"It's possible that my dear friend here has been deliberately avoiding nightmares related to all this." Claudia chuckled and gently patted the Pan-Dora's activation hilt. "I don't know if she's simply trying to be a nuisance or whether she has some other goal."

"...You know, I've been thinking this for a while, but I'm amazed how you can keep using that Orga Lux, Claudia," Sylvia said, her voice ringing with awe.

"Oh? She's rather adorable, once you get to know her. And well...it would be tough to go up against opponents like what we're about to face without her power."

Indeed, the Varda-Vaos was known to possess considerable fighting potential even without drawing on its main ability. While it wasn't quite at Lamina Mortis's level, Ayato himself had fought it, and in skill, it was comparable to the top-ranked students at each of Asterisk's six schools. Of course, that wasn't accounting for outliers like Orphelia or Xinglou.

"Those abilities really are a nuisance though, aren't they?" Sylvia, having fought against them once herself, looked pained.

"U-um... I know it's a little late to suggest this, but is there any way Stjarnagarm could help out...?" This came from Kirin, her face awash with worry. "At least Commander Helga and Haruka. They already know everything anyway..."

"I considered that, of course, but I don't think we can risk it," Claudia answered with a shake of her head. "The Golden Bough Alliance is already on guard, first against foundations, and second against Commander Helga and the Ban'yuu Tenra, both of whom are equivalent in power to Erenshkigal. I don't know about the latter, but I'm quite sure they're watching Commander Helga. Especially given what we learned this morning."

Taking everything into account, there was a clear implication that someone within the city guard was feeding the Golden Bough Alliance information, even if unwillingly. It was only natural to assume that it wasn't only those officers responsible for patrolling the city who had been influenced by the Varda-Vaos.

"Even Erenshkigal said they have people within Stjarnagarm," Saya added in agreement. "I doubt she was lying."

"Lamina Mortis is obsessed with Haruka, too, so I suspect she'll be under increased surveillance as well. She won't be completely free to act without drawing attention to herself. For that matter, it's probably safe to assume that our own actions are being monitored, at least to some extent. Isn't that right, Ayato?"

"Yeah. When I fought Lamina Mortis alongside Haruka, he seemed to have a good grasp of what we were doing."

"The strategy this time, so to speak, lies in how many pieces we can put into play without tipping off our adversaries. We need to fly under their radar. Let's say the allowable limit is ten points, and each of us is worth ten—with six of us, that's sixty points. But Haruka and Commander Helga are worth at least twice as much as us—perhaps even three or five times... If we make a poor play, it will be game over then and there." Claudia paused, spreading her hands wide for emphasis.

"I guess it depends how much they want to stick to their original timing, but I agree we can't afford to underestimate them. Any mistakes would be irreversible," Saya added with a frown.

Their original timing... According to Orphelia, that was immediately after the championship match...

"We have three trump cards up our sleeves. First, we know what the Golden Bough Alliance is planning—or at least what Erenshkigal's role in it is. Second, we know the whereabouts of two of their leaders. And lastly, the Golden Bough Alliance is unaware of the first two points."

Indeed, only seven individuals—the six of them present plus Julis—knew what they knew. There was no way the Golden Bough Alliance could be aware.

"Without these three elements, our strategy would be unconscionably reckless. Which is to say our adversaries can't possibly be expecting us to try it. For that reason, we can't afford to let this advantage go to waste."

"Ugh... I think I get it. So we're going to have to go all out...!" Kirin, seemingly on the verge of tears, pressed her hands firmly together, when—

"Well, we've arrived. That's enough discussion, I think."

The car had just turned in to the underground parking lot at Hotel Elnath. From here, they would split into three groups.

"Be careful, everyone," Claudia said once they had stepped outside, her face brimming with confidence. "Let's give it our best. There's no need for concern—we can do this."

After watching Eishirou vanish in a puff of smoke like the ninja he was, followed by Ayato and the others departing the underground parking lot, Sylvia caught Claudia with a sideways glance.

"*Don't worry? We can do this...?* You sure seem certain," she said.

"What of it?"

"I was just wondering what you think our chances are, following this strategy of yours."

Claudia fell silent for a moment, before finally letting out a weak sigh. "Well... You can weigh up the variables a few ways, but no matter how you cut it, I wouldn't give us more than twenty percent. Probably closer to around ten at best."

"I thought so," Sylvia said with a dry chuckle, glancing skyward. "The biggest bottleneck is that we don't know where the Tyrant is, right?"

"That's right. But also...Lamina Mortis and the Varda-Vaos are still unknown to us as opponents. And we don't know what those thousand-plus autonomous puppets are up to—or Agrestia for that matter. There are too many elements to make an accurate calculation," Claudia said with a tired drop of her shoulders.

And yet—

"But we've got to do what we've got to do, right?"

"...Yes, of course."

The two young women exchanged measured glances, their expressions warming.

"Say, Claudia? I've got an idea."

"Oh? What is it?"

"I'd like to call in a helper."

"...A helper? Now?"

"*What on earth are you talking about?*" her expression all but asked.

"Additional help would be invaluable, but as I mentioned earlier, the conditions we're operating under are incredibly strict. We can't afford to tip off our adversaries. And if this help is only halfway competent, they could end up being a liability. At the very least, they would have to be a Page One or around that level. And, of course, they would have to be someone the Golden Bough Alliance doesn't already view as a threat. Which is all to say that they would need to be among the best fighters in their school, willing to plough ahead unquestioningly even if it puts their own life on the line, and someone who has gone unnoticed by our adversaries thus far... It wouldn't be easy to find someone who fits all those criteria."

"I already have. Give me a minute." Sylvia took out her mobile and quickly dialed in a call. "Besides, she's already related to all this. I'd like to let her join us if we can. We don't need to explain the whole situation... Ah, it's connecting."

An air-window slid open in front of her, revealing a familiar face.

"...*Sylvia? Um, is something the matter?*"

"I see...," Claudia said beside her with a short nod.

"Yeah, I need to ask you something... Will you hear me out, Minato?"

*

It was almost noon.

Proceeding down the dimly lit passageway, Julis stopped to take a deep breath.

A little farther ahead, the gate was overflowing with dazzling light.

It was time.

At long last, it was time.

She almost found herself looking back on the long days that had led up to this, but suddenly stopped.

There was no need for such sentimentality now.

Everything would be fine once the battle was over.

Reaffirming her determination, she stepped forward.

"Here it is, here it is! To uncontrollable excitement, uncontrollable passions, uncontrollable applause, the long-awaited finale to this year's incredible Lindvolus! Having overcome countless formidable opponents, Seidoukan Academy's fifth-ranked fighter is emerging now from the East Gate! As a Strega, her skills are second to none, unparalleled! With her ability to freely manipulate flowers of pure flame, she's certainly worthy of the title Glühen Rose! In the fifth round, our indomitable blossom emerged victorious against Jie Long Seventh Institute's Hagun Seikun, and in the semifinal she defeated

her own tag team partner, Seidoukan's number one, the Murakumo, Ayato Amagiri! Now, hoping to snatch only the second grand slam in the entire history of the Festa, here she is at last! Julis-Alexia von Riessfeld!"

The audience erupted in a deafening roar as she entered the stage.

This was the third time she had reached the final match in the Festa, but never before had the atmosphere felt so intense. It was positively blistering, the heat so extreme that she thought for a second her skin might literally burn. The excitement was incredible—insane even—the vibrations coursing through the air so powerful that they alone might end up laying waste to the Sirius Dome.

She kept her gaze fixed straight ahead as she made her way across the bridge that led down to the stage.

Her counterpart had yet to appear through the arena's opposite gate.

Until now, she had always been able to bring herself to acknowledge the audience's cheers with a casual wave, but today was different.

This fight belonged to her and Orphelia.

...Except that isn't right, she corrected herself with a shake of her head.

There was no doubt that this contest was between her and Orphelia, but she still had Ayato and the rest of her friends backing her up.

No sooner did Julis reach the stage than a thunderous roar sounded from the audience, surpassing her wildest expectations.

"And now! Yes, now, here she is emerging from the West Gate! The absolute favorite with the official odds at one point one in her favor! Our defending champion, undefeated in every battle—official and unofficial—since she first stepped foot in Asterisk! The Supreme Queen that not even Sigrdrífa, the great Sylvia Lyyneheym, hoping to avenge her previous defeat, could overcome! The strongest of all Stregas, having overpowered every last challenger with her indomitable

power! Her deadly toxins can overwhelm even Orga Luxes! If her opponent is aiming to secure a grand slam, then she's gunning to be the first-ever winner of three separate Lindvoli! Le Wolfe Black Institute's number one! The Witch of Solitary Venom, Erenshkigal, Orphelia Landlufen!"

Despite this grand introduction, Orphelia's look was as sorrowful as ever, her gait characteristically resigned as she made her way slowly down from the bridge to the stage below.

"You came, Orphelia," Julis called out after switching off her microphone.

"You too, Julis." Orphelia's response was, surprisingly, immediate.

"Is it me, or do you look a little agitated? That isn't like you."

"...No, it isn't. Perhaps I am." Orphelia's crimson eyes remained locked on Julis. "To be honest, I didn't expect your fate to be this strong. To think that it has a chance of standing up to mine."

"Ha! Don't mock me, Orphelia. It isn't thanks to *fate* that I'm standing here before you. It's thanks to my abilities," Julis called back, meeting her opponent's gaze head-on.

"It makes no difference to me... But very well. Show me what you're capable of."

All at once, Orphelia's prana swelled with explosive force.

"...!"

It was too overwhelming, that raw onslaught of power.

This was her fourth fight with Orphelia, but Julis felt that her foe was immeasurably stronger now than she had been during those past encounters. She had fought countless commanding opponents thus far, but Orphelia was without a doubt the most powerful.

Julis knew that. She had known it from the very beginning.

She almost took an instinctive step backward, but stopped herself, standing her ground.

This was a bluff on her part, a false show of force brought on by unseemly, crude tenacity.

And yet—

"I'll say it again. Don't mock me, Orphelia."

"…" Wordlessly, Orphelia turned her back on Julis and made her way to her starting position.

The stage, Julis noticed, was already encased behind its shield of protective gel.

It was time to begin.

By now, Ayato and the others would have already gotten underway.

All Julis had to focus on was doing what she had come here to do—*finishing* what she had come here to finish.

"I'm going to take it back! All of it! *That's* why I'm here!" she called out.

"Good." Orphelia responded without so much as turning around, her voice tinged with sadness. "And I'll put an end to everything. That's why *I'm* here."

The next moment, an artificial voice announced the opening of the match:

"Lindvolus Championship Match—begin!"

CHAPTER 6
THE HOLY LANCE

The dim corridors of Asterisk's underground block were illuminated at regular intervals, but the total amount of light was far from sufficient to see properly. In that darkness, three shadows pushed forward, their footfalls echoing around them.

The lead shadow—Ayato—came to a stop once more. Staring straight ahead, he lifted his hand to urge Saya and Kirin to likewise come to a halt.

A short distance ahead, the passageway split into three.

He zoomed in on the air-window displaying the map that Claudia had prepared in advance. Comparing the layout of the passages to their current location, the rightmost one looked to be the most promising.

And yet—

Slowly, he closed his eyes, calmed his nerves, and used the Amagiri Shinmei style's perception-increasing *shiki* technique to explore his surroundings.

Then, concentrating his attention on the middle part between two of the passages, he realized that what had seemed at first no more than a blank wall was in reality a stagnant flow of concentrated mana.

Cutting through that mass with the Ser Veresta, he felt the air become suddenly lighter.

Then, checking the map once more, he saw the correct route to be the one on the left.

"Phew..."

Exhaling deeply, he sheathed the Ser Veresta. Saya spoke up in exasperation behind him: "Good grief... Another one?"

More than an hour had passed since the three of them had entered the underground block. If they were where they thought they were, this was close to the elevator leading up to the Festa stage.

The underground block, with its mesh of passageways and drainage channels, was a veritable labyrinth. Yet in spite of that, the area was well maintained, and with the help of a map, they weren't likely to get lost, even if the journey did take a little time.

Unless, that was, traps had been set up to mislead and misdirect them, as had been the case just now.

These were probably—well, almost certainly—the work of the Varda-Vaos. At first, they had failed to notice these diversions, set at seemingly every crossroads, and had been sent meandering all over the place.

"Let's go...!" Ayato took off at a run. Saya and Kirin nodded in agreement and followed after him.

For a while, the path proceeded straight ahead. Ayato wasn't about to let down his guard, but he doubted this was another ruse like the previous ones.

"W-we need to hurry...!" Kirin exclaimed anxiously as she glanced at the time. "The match has already started...!"

It was already noon.

"Don't worry...! Once we get through here, we should be just about...!"

Before Ayato could finish speaking, the path ahead of him opened up.

"Huh...?"

Grinding to a halt, he took in his surroundings.

They had reached a huge domed space, an area around ten meters high and fifty in diameter that didn't resemble an underground cavern in the slightest. It wasn't quite as large as the Festa stage, but it was still immense.

There was no indication of this area on the map. Instead, the evidence of its recent construction was piled up along the walls in mounds of rubble. It could only have been formed by merging three separate levels—and indeed, glancing up, Ayato saw higher passages opening out onto the walls, and water cascading down from drainage channels whose paths had been severed.

"This place…!"

Ayato and Kirin immediately went into high alert.

And then—

"So you came after all," a bright, knowing voice echoed.

Stepping out from one of those many broken passageways was a young woman dressed in a men's black military uniform—Agrestia, Saint Gallardworth Academy's fifth-ranking fighter and the wielder of the Orga Lux the Amalthean Goat, part of the Life Rhodes's Team Lancelot, whom Ayato had fought in the deciding match of the Phoenix.

"…Percival Gardner," Saya murmured.

Ayato had heard that Percival was now working for the Golden Bough Alliance from Kirin, who had fought her in the lakeside city. But seeing it for himself…

"There are three elevators leading up to the Festa stage that still function. You won't be able to reach any of them without passing through here," Percival said plainly as she continued her approach.

A huge chalice-shaped Orga Lux was floating in the upper-right corner of the hall, growing brighter by the second.

"But it will be quite impossible for you to take even one more step forward."

"We don't have time for this. We'll force our way through," Ayato said, readying the Ser Veresta while Saya activated her Helnekraum and Kirin readied her Hiinamaru sword in a fighting stance.

Percival was looking their way, but her eyes were black and stagnant, reflecting nothing at all. She seemed completely different than she had during their previous encounters—empty, as though a deep darkness lurked beneath the surface...

"...Ayato." Saya, no doubt having noticed it too, tugged at his sleeve.

"Yeah, I know."

This had to be the work of the Varda-Vaos. Its habit of turning people into puppets was nothing short of horrifying.

"There was something strange about her when I fought her last time, but she wasn't like this..." Kirin, though on guard, seemed pained by the sight before her.

Percival closed her eyes. In a cold, mechanical voice, she intoned: *"I am your gun and nothing more. I will take the sins of destroying your enemies unto myself."*

When her eyes finally snapped open, a burst of golden light spilled forth from the Amalthean Goat.

"A halo of mercy and atonement I give unto thee."

That light would deprive its targets of consciousness with the slightest touch, so Ayato was forced to lash out against it with the Ser Veresta.

"Auuuuurgggggghhhhh!"

With a terrible roar from Ayato, the Ser Veresta caught the torrent of light and tore straight through it.

The last time he had tried this, the strain had taken a considerable toll on the weapon. Now, however, he had attained a new level of mastery with the Orga Lux. He wasn't about to be outmatched, not even by the Holy Grail.

Eventually, the light dissipated, and Ayato swung the Ser Veresta once more to dispel any remaining residue, before turning it next on Percival. "Sorry about this, but it's three against one. We're going to push past you!"

Percival was a tough opponent and, according to Kirin, much faster on her feet now than she had been during the Gryps. But even so, she was alone against Ayato, Kirin, and Saya. She couldn't hope to stop all three of them.

And of course, the Amalthean Goat, while certainly powerful, needed to be charged for a certain length of time between each use. She wouldn't be able to keep on attacking with it in rapid succession.

Nonetheless, Percival didn't seem to be in any hurry. "It isn't three against one," she said, raising her right hand into the air. "It's a hundred against three."

"…!"

At that moment, more autonomous puppets than one could count emerged from the various broken passageways.

"Valiants…!"

Just as Kirin had reported, they did indeed look like Ardy—and while individually, their specifications weren't quite so impressive, together…

"I wasn't expecting this many of them…" Saya, standing back-to-back with Ayato, furrowed her brow as she took in the scene.

The three of them were already completely surrounded.

In that case, it was probably safe to assume this whole cavern had been constructed to provide a space to overwhelm them through force of numbers.

He hadn't been able to count the puppets himself, but if Percival was to be believed, there were a hundred of them in total. Ernesta claimed to have delivered a thousand units overall, so this would constitute a full 10 percent of their numbers.

"No matter how many you are, no one goes any further," Percival's voice echoed from beyond the Valiants.

At that moment, the puppets themselves each activated hammer-shaped Luxes, readying themselves for combat.

"Uh-oh…! This could be a problem…!"

Dodging the first oncoming swing of a hammer, Ayato lashed out with the Ser Veresta to cut the Valiant down, then kicked away two more that came rushing toward him in tandem to take advantage of the momentary opening. Their defensive barriers blocked his attack, but he used those shields as footholds to leap higher, twisting in midair as he swung the Ser Veresta to remove both units' heads.

"Ba-doom...!"

Saya's voice was more spirited than usual as the bullets of light firing from her Helnekraum exploded on impact with the multi-layered defensive barriers deployed by the Valiants.

"Nggghhh...!"

Though not as robust as Ardy's defensive shields, when deployed in layers from multiple units, not even Saya's immense firepower was enough to break through them. Nor did the Valiants themselves leave any openings to counter. There were simply too many. If the three of them were separated somehow and this battle devolved into a melee, they would be at a severe disadvantage.

Using the feedback from his perception-expanding state of *shiki* to guide him, Ayato noticed the circle of Valiants was thinnest in the vicinity of the passage the three of them had just used to enter the room... It might be possible to break through and then defeat the puppets one by one in the narrow passage.

That, however, could end up taking too much time.

Right now, their highest priority had to be reaching Lamina Mortis as quickly as possible.

"...Ayato, Saya," Kirin whispered as she dodged attacks from multiple Valiants. "I'll use the Fudaraku. Leap out of the way when I draw my blade."

"..."

Ayato and Saya exchanged silent nods.

With that, Kirin took a step forward and returned the Hiinamaru to its scabbard, drawing in its place a second blade from her right hip—the katana-shaped Orga Lux known as Fudaraku.

The Fudaraku's uniqueness lay in its ability to store energy— the more energy it accumulated, the sharper and more powerful the weapon became.

As Kirin sheathed her blade, five Valiants saw their opportunity and attempted to close in on her, hammers raised.

"...Here I come."

Ayato and Saya leaped back as those words escaped Kirin's lips—and at that moment, a silver circle of light flashed around her in all directions.

As Kirin began to unsheathe the Fudaraku, its silver glow overflowed. The brilliant burst of light emanated out from her, freezing the Valiants as though time itself had ground to a halt.

"That's..."

As Ayato and Saya landed back on the ground, the bodies of the surrounding Valiants gradually collapsed—then exploded.

That single burst of light had split them clean in two.

All one hundred of them.

"Wow...," Saya murmured, incredulous as the explosions rang out around them.

The Fudaraku's blade was composed of metal, not light, and while it gave off an incredible reflective sheen, it was wholly shaped like a Japanese katana. Nonetheless, its terrifying latent power was no doubt capable of overwhelming even the Ser Veresta. With the energy Kirin had stored inside it over all this time, there could be no withstanding its full force.

"I see... So that's the Fudaraku. Phenomenal." A frigid voice came across the flames left from the explosions. "You're dangerous. D's assessment was correct. I'll have to eliminate you here, no matter what it takes."

"...You sound pretty relaxed, given the situation," Saya interjected, stepping forward and aiming the Helnekraum at her target.

"Relaxed...? I don't think so. I'm always doing my best. How else could I hope to atone...? Ah, yes, I see. I suppose I was being deceptive before. I wasn't truly facing my sins. Let me atone for that, too, here and now." Percival's vacant eyes widened as she lifted her right hand high into the air.

Then, responding to her, the Amalthean Goat floating in the upper-right part of the hall began to change form. The Orga Lux, shaped like a chalice tilted on its side, started to stretch long and thin, encircling the thorns decorating its bottom half.

"It can't be...!"

Saya was the first to react—squeezing the trigger of the Helnekraum and firing at the all-but-defenseless Percival.

Her aim was perfect. With a tremendous roar, a fresh explosion erupted, the blast clearing away the wreckage of the fallen Valiants still burning throughout the hall.

And yet—

Percival was no longer there, reappearing instead in one of the broken passageways two levels above.

In her hands, she was grasping a spear, distorted like a thorn stretched beyond recognition.

When did she...? How did she manage to dodge Saya's attack just now...?

"*Ngh*... So it *is* the Holy Lance," Saya murmured, her disappointment clear as she glanced up at Percival.

"The Holy Lance?" Kirin repeated, coming up next to her.

"There were rumors, that the Holy Grail—the Amalthean Goat—has a secret second form," Saya continued without letting Percival out of her sights. "I thought they were bogus. But there it is. The Holy Lance. The IEFs have to publish their data on their urm-manadite stocks, so just about anyone can get a rough idea of their capabilities. One researcher looking over the data came up with a hypothesis—that it might be possible to reverse the Amalthean Goat's abilities if its user's compatibility rate passed a certain level. But it was just a rumor. The Holy Lance has never actually been used in battle, and I didn't take it seriously, either..."

They had deployed extensive countermeasures against the Amalthean Goat during the Gryps, but neither Claudia nor Saya had mentioned anything like this back then. In other words, those rumors must not have seemed very credible at the time.

"If it reverses its abilities, does that mean its attacks will change…?"

The Amalthean Goat's ability was known as *soul removal*. It had no physical attack power, but to make up for that, it rendered any who touched its light instantly unconscious. So the reverse of that would have to be—

"*Pierce, O Light of Judgment!*"

"…!"

Percival lashed out with the Holy Lance, shooting a laser-like beam of light right at Ayato and the others.

The three of them quickly dodged, but the light carved straight into the ground, tearing through the floor.

"Right. So that's its technique reversed."

Its radiance now seemed to be composed of heightened physical-attack power.

That, however, was something that they could deal with. In fact, it was almost a relief that its most dangerous elements had been reduced to just a weapon.

Until the very next moment, at least.

"Ayato, watch out!"

"What…?!"

Percival rushed forward all at once, aiming straight for Ayato as he dodged her previous attack. Given her extraordinary speed, she almost skewered him straight through the abdomen.

It was a lightning-fast thrust—followed by another, and another, all in rapid succession.

"Too fast…!"

But the speed wasn't all—each blow was also unusually heavy, and though he caught them all with the Ser Veresta, the repeated shocks were unmistakably wearing down his defensive posture.

It wasn't raw strength, either—yes, the Holy Lance did have significant power output, but something about it was simply *wrong*.

How is it managing to push the Ser Veresta to the brink…?!

"*Burst, O Light of Judgment!*"

"*Ugh…!*"

He had thought he avoided the blow but was knocked to the ground as the golden light momentarily swelled and threw him back.

It was strong.

And it posed a serious threat.

It wasn't quite at the level of Julis's *Queen of the Night*, but there was no doubt that it was in the same class as Gigoku's *shikigami* syncretism.

Indeed, this Percival was completely different to the one whom he had fought during the Gryps.

"*Scour, O Light of Judgment!*"

With those words, the Holy Lance unleashed a myriad of fine, bullet-like projectiles.

"Amagiri Shinmei Sword Style—*Three-Legged Crow!*"

Ayato deflected that barrage with the Ser Veresta, but Percival proceeded to hold the Holy Lance high in the air as it continued to unleash its light.

Uh-oh…! I won't be able to avoid that one…!

"Ayato!" Saya's bitter cry rang out as Percival's next strike bore down on his throat—

"Hah!"

In the nick of time, Kirin intervened with her Fudaraku, parrying the Holy Lance.

"Ayato! Saya! Please, you need to go…!" she cried, her voice coming with difficulty as she engaged Percival in fierce battle.

"We can't leave you! It will take all three of us to beat her…!" Saya protested.

"But our goal isn't to beat *her*!" Kirin called back. "You two have a more important foe! Leave this to me!"

"…"

Ayato was about to object, but his words caught in his throat at the sight of her determination.

She was right, of course.

They had come here to defeat Lamina Mortis, to put an end to his rampage.

Naturally, they would have a better chance of beating Percival if the three of them fought together. However, they would be unlikely to emerge unscathed, and the longer they took, the closer this whole operation would come to failure. After all, even with the three of them, it would be difficult to defeat her as she was now in any reasonable amount of time.

"I'll be fine…! Besides, I won before, didn't I?" Kirin said, glancing at Ayato with a mischievous smile.

She was referring to their semifinal match during the Gryps when she had fought against Xiaohui Wu.

Ayato and Kirin, while engaging him together, had been unable to deal any serious blows. Kirin, however, underwent an explosive burst of growth and finally snatched victory.

"…All right."

Given the situation, he had no choice now but to trust her, as he had back then.

"Let's go, Saya!"

"B-but… *Nnnnnngh*…! Fine! You can do it, Kirin!" Saya still seemed unconvinced, her jaw clenched in worry. But in the end, she followed after Ayato.

"I can't let you pass." With those words, Percival repelled Kirin and directed the Holy Lance against Ayato and Saya.

Its golden light grew brighter still, but just before she could release it, a sideways strike threw her hard against the wall.

"…!"

Kirin, armed with the Fudaraku, called out after her: "Didn't you hear me? *I'm* your opponent."

*

A year and a half earlier, during a meeting on an airship…

"So you want to bring her into the fold…? Hmm. It's not like you to make that kind of suggestion."

Madiath rubbed his chin in thought as he took in the image of Percival's face projected by the air-window.

The only time the members of the Golden Bough Alliance met in person like this was when there was something of considerable importance to discuss.

"I wouldn't have expected to hear this from you, seeing how you were opposed to our efforts to recruit Xinglou Fan," Varda remarked, watching Madiath with her head tilted to one side.

She wasn't being ironic—she was no doubt simply pointing out a fact. Nonetheless, the observation roused Dirk's ire.

"Not as an ally. Just a pawn," he replied, making no effort to conceal his frustration as he stared back at Varda and scratched his cheek. "But a talented pawn, the kind you don't often come across. Certainly worth the effort it would take to bring her in."

"The effort, yes...," Madiath repeated. He clearly had something more to say.

"...What's the problem?" Dirk asked with a murderous stare.

"Oh, I was just thinking how you seem willing to go to considerable lengths for this *outstanding* resource of yours." Madiath gave an exaggerated shrug. "Ranked number five at Gallardworth, the wielder of the Holy Grail. A highly accurate shooter, eyes capable of seeing through deception, a perfect rearguard fighter... Yes, she does indeed look excellent. She's certainly earned the alias Agrestia. But...is it enough to embrace her as one of us?"

"I agree," Varda added. "There is no mistaking Percival Gardner's abilities, but if we were concerned with abilities alone, there would be countless other candidates. Even if we needed more pawns, there is no clear reason why we should choose her."

As Dirk had expected, the two were unified in their opposition.

That, however, couldn't be helped. At Gallardworth, Percival had always dedicated herself to serving as part of a team. You could watch a recording of any of her matches, and it would be enough to demonstrate her worthiness as a Page One. However...

"Hmph. Neither of you have a shred of discernment." Dirk scoffed, sending additional data to Madiath and Varda's terminals.

"And this is…?"

"Data from when I had her on *my* team at the Institute."

The two fell silent for a moment as they took in the information.

Varda spoke up first: "Oh? So she's an irregular designer child? This is certainly intriguing, but is it enough to stand out?"

At this, Dirk let out an exaggerated sigh. "You're a machine, an Orga Lux through and through. You can't see the intrinsic worth of human beings. If you don't get it, just shut up for a minute, would you?"

Madiath, meanwhile, continued to stare at the air-window for a moment longer. Finally, his lips twisted in a grin, he looked up. "Ah… I see what you mean."

As Dirk had expected, *he* had noticed it.

"As far as I can see, this data doesn't paint a very different image from her record at Gallardworth. She's an excellent backup fighter, with a particularly outstanding shooting ability. But it *is* strange…"

"…? What is?" Varda asked, even now still stumbling in the dark.

"Oh, it's all very simple," Madiath explained gently, like a teacher lecturing a child. "According to what's written here, the Institute was trying to genetically engineer designer babies with the same specifications as Genestella. She's the result born from that process—a genetically engineered Genestella."

"I can see that. It explains why her physical capabilities are above those of other designer children…," Varda remarked, before quickly shifting her attention to Dirk.

"Heh. So you finally caught on?"

"Genetic engineering is a technology from a bygone age, and she's probably the only Genestella to have been produced by it," Madiath explained. "So why did she devote herself to serving as a rearguard supporting fighter?"

Indeed.

Percival Gardner's true domain was close-quarters combat.

The fact that she had survived a direct confrontation against Rodolfo Zoppo was proof enough of that.

"Wait. Are you saying Percival Gardner, whether as part of Dirk's team or at Gallardworth, has never demonstrated her true potential?" Varda asked.

"Nah, that ain't quite right." Dirk shook his head. "Watching her teammates get annihilated came as a pretty big blow to her. Since then, she's held back from close combat. No matter how I threatened or coddled her, she wouldn't give me the time of day."

That had been a major miscalculation on his part, as he had been the one who recruited her. She was certainly good enough in the rearguard, but he couldn't see it as anything short of a shame to put her true talents to waste.

Now, however...

"Maybe *you* can do something about that, Varda?"

"...So that is what you meant by *effort*. I'd rather you didn't place the burden on me for such things, but..." Varda seemed taken aback, but didn't deny it could be done.

"So do you have a plan in mind to draw her in?" Madiath asked.

"Does that mean you are in favor of this idea?" Varda rejoindered.

"Oh yes. We're most definitely short on manpower, and if this works out, it would be an interesting hidden play to keep on hand should anything go wrong."

"Okay. I'll get her to come here, then. Won't be a problem," Dirk said.

Percival wanted to destroy the Institute, but even if she did manage to win at the Festa, it would hardly grant her wish. Strictly speaking, the organization *could* be crushed, but a successor would simply be created in short order to take its place.

All he had to do was exploit that fact, and he would easily win her over. At the very least, it would be enough to get her to hear him out. Then, with Varda there to help, everything would take off without a hitch.

"I don't wish to increase my burden, but I will accept that she seems a valuable resource. This will be a conditional agreement."

Varda didn't seem particularly enthusiastic, but she *had* given in.

"What conditions?"

"Percival Gardner's fighting ability is presently unclear. Until it is clarified, I cannot give my full support."

Well, that was fair enough.

"You're welcome to test her yourself if you want. But if I had to guess..." Dirk paused for a second, then flashed his counterpart his usual easygoing grin. "She might even be stronger than you are now."

*

"Ugh...!"

Somehow, Kirin managed to bring the Fudaraku around in time to repel Percival's thrust, careening at an almost godlike speed.

Yet by the time she managed to bring her blade back around to counter, Percival had already backed away.

Not only that, the tip of the Holy Lance was glowing once more, and a golden light burst from the ground at her feet like an erupting geyser.

"Ascend, O Light of Judgment!"

Kirin raced to avoid the attack, but several pillars of light erupted from the earth in pursuit, forcing her to leap up into one of the broken passages looming from the second floor of the hall.

"Haah... Haah...!"

She had known it would be the case, but Percival was indeed strong—completely different to how she had been during their fight in the lakeside city.

To begin with, her foe's speed was unrecognizable—an order of magnitude faster. Not even Xiaohui Wu, whom Kirin had fought during the Gryps, had improved to this extent. If not for her eyes, capable of channeling her prana to gauge her opponent's next moves, she would have fallen victim to the Holy Lance in no time at all. It wasn't just a matter of offensive and defensive techniques— it was like her foe now inhabited a completely different plane of existence.

And then there was the golden light being emitted by the Holy Lance. Unlike in its Holy Grail form, the light didn't rob its target of consciousness in a single blow, but rather manifested as a wide range of attack forms, each of them potent and powerful. Kirin suspected if she had Ayato's strength she might have been able to withstand them, but as she was, even a single blow would probably be enough to spell her demise.

But that doesn't mean I can just fall back…!

Reaffirming her spirit and resolve, she sped past the burning remains of the Valiants spread left and right throughout the hall and closed in on Percival.

"Kyargh!"

Percival parried her slash with the Holy Lance, meeting her weapon not with the side of her own blade, but with its tip. Kirin followed through, attacking from above, sweeping up from below, thrusting from the front—but her foe stopped each attempt the same way. During their last encounter, Percival had exchanged blows with Kirin's blade using her gun-type Luxes, but this time, she was holding Kirin back with astonishingly precise movements.

For her part, Percival's eyes could see through pretense and falsehood, which rendered Kirin's Toudou-style Hidden Technique, her Conjoined Cranes, ineffective. Since feints were useless, her only choice was to go all out from the front.

"Rage, O Light of Judgment!"

The golden light swirled like a gust of wind, quickly buffeting Kirin as she shielded herself with the Fudaraku.

Her attack canceled and momentum disrupted, Kirin was left at a distinct disadvantage.

"Hah!" She tried to break through the interval by releasing her sword energy, but the strike was easily evaded.

Well, she had suspected as much. Through those slashes, she might have been able to release projectiles of a sort, but in the end, they were simply flying tools. Such a technique would hardly prove effective against Percival in her current state—unless, of course, it was employed with particular finesse.

"Pursue, O Light of Judgment!"

At that moment, several bands of light shot out from the Holy Lance, launching straight for Kirin.

She ran to avoid them, but the strips of light changed trajectory midflight in chase.

Homing attacks...?!

They were probably similar to Saya's homing blaster, the Waldenholt Mark II.

Kirin's sole option was to hold her ground and lash out with the Fudaraku, but of course Percival immediately capitalized on that opening to close in with a series of perfectly targeted thrusts straight for her throat, her heart, her stomach, only backing off when Kirin sidestepped to launch her own counterattack.

"...!"

At its most basic, Percival's strategy relied on using the Holy Lance to establish a favorable distance between the two adversaries, and once an opportunity presented itself, to dash forward and launch into a close-quarters melee attack. But she never overplayed her hand, and she never got too close. It was a solid tactic, one that offered no means to turn the tables on her.

But that doesn't mean I don't have a chance...!

Overall, Percival was the far superior opponent, but that didn't mean she had Kirin beat on every front.

First, there was technical ability. Percival was clearly competent at employing Saint Gallardworth Academy's various spear techniques, but she wasn't yet an expert. Of course, each blow was precisely targeted and packed considerable power, and she fought with formidable speed, but it seemed also that she hadn't quite perfected her technique through long training; she fought only at the level of one who understood the underlying theory. The old Kirin would have been hard-pressed to respond, but with her current knowledge, she could hold her opponent off without fear.

Her other advantage was the Fudaraku. It was said that with one month's worth of stored sword energy, it was capable of competing head-to-head with even one of the Four Colored Runeswords. With four months' worth of reserve, no Orga Lux should be able to defeat it.

No doubt Percival herself was aware of these two points, as she hadn't yet attempted to finish Kirin off in a sustained close-quarters attack.

Still...

"*Rend, O Light of Judgment!*"

With a sweep of the Holy Lance, Percival unleashed a burst of light faster than anything else thus far.

Kirin raced to dodge it with a forward roll, only for the strike to gouge a gaping gash in the wall above her.

And with each additional swing of the Holy Lance, more and more such attacks came speeding toward her.

"Haah, haah...!"

If she allowed herself to get distracted even for a moment, she would be sliced clean in two, and so she continued to evade, her breath ragged. Percival's breathing, however, wasn't in the least disturbed.

I won't be able to take my chance if this keeps up...! At best, I might have one or two opportunities...!

Desperate, she continued to dodge the oncoming bands of light, occasionally parrying them with the Fudaraku, simply enduring as she waited for her chance to hit back.

And then—

Percival, perhaps having sensed that Kirin's movements were slowing, pressed forward once again.

Thus far, she had demonstrated a habit of using more thrust

attacks than slashes. That being the case, she would likely do the same again this time.

Even with her clairvoyance, Kirin wouldn't have been able to move in time after reading her foe's next moves. If she missed her chance, death awaited her.

But against this opponent, she wouldn't stand a chance of winning if she wasn't prepared to take that risk.

Percival homed another thrust in on a single point. Instead of falling back, Kirin dared to step forward, letting lose an upward slash of the Fudaraku as she shifted her body.

"…!"

Almost at the exact same moment, the Holy Lance grazed her flank—but it was only a shallow wound.

Kirin, however, didn't waste a moment reacting. Percival instantly rotated her body to avoid the oncoming strike. The Fudaraku tore through her military uniform, sending a long piece of cloth flapping to the ground and exposing Percival's toned body as a faint red line ran across her abdomen.

How did she manage to avoid that…?

Falling back this time, Kirin clicked her tongue, amazed by Percival's physical ability.

"…"

Her foe, on the other hand, glanced down at her stomach with dark eyes, then slowly turned her gaze back to Kirin. She didn't seem perturbed in the slightest.

"I see. It seems I still underestimated you. In that case…you leave me…n-no choice…"

"…?"

All of a sudden, Percival's words stuttered—yet her facial expression remained as stolid as ever.

Kirin, however, couldn't afford to dwell on that mystery.

"S-slaughter, O Light of Judgment!"

Percival braced herself with the Holy Lance held out before her as an unusual amount of light began to spill from the weapon's tip.

This was bad.

Very bad.

Suppressing the instinctive wave of fear that washed over her, Kirin leaped high into the air.

"Holy Lance—fire!"

From the weapon's tip, a golden torrent similar to the Holy Grail's energy wave began to spill out.

Kirin managed to evade the deluge just before it could reach her by kicking off from the ceiling, but she was thrown across the hall by the aftershock and knocked to her back as she hit the ground.

"Gah…!"

But the sight of what came next sent the pain of her landing far into the periphery of her senses.

Flying through the air, the flood of light that had targeted her tore through every level of the underground block—even ripping through the clouds that covered the sky above.

That destructive power was nothing short of incredible.

And an even more unbelievable sight yet awaited her:

"Rise, O Light of Judgment!"

"What…?!"

She's using it a second time…?!

But it should have been too soon for that.

Percival readied the Holy Lance in the same position as before, its golden glow increasing once again.

Uh-oh…! I won't be able to dodge it from this position…!

The next moment, the ensuing torrent of light swallowed Kirin whole.

*

"…The Holy Grail's second form?" Laetitia Blanchard asked, raising her eyebrows as she sipped her cup of tea. "You said you had something to discuss, but why this all of a sudden?"

Laetitia was the former vice president of the student council at Saint Gallardworth Academy, but although she was presently sitting in the familiar student council room, the council was under new leadership, and all official duties ought to have been their responsibility, not hers.

The new president, Elliot Forster, wore a strained expression from his seat behind his desk.

"Of course, I've read the data," he answered. "But there are some things I can't quite wrap my head around looking at that alone..."

"Did you find something in connection to Percival, perhaps?"

Percival Gardner was a close friend and the current user of the Holy Grail, whose whereabouts were presently unknown. Given the situation, any inquiry about the Holy Grail would *have* to be in relation to her.

Yet as Laetitia watched him from her seat on the guest sofa, Elliot quietly shook his head. "No, it isn't like that. But you were close to Gardner, weren't you? I was hoping you might be able to offer us a clue as to what's going on."

"..."

She couldn't tell whether his intentions were honest or deceitful. It certainly seemed that Elliot had taken a few tricks of the trade to heart.

When he had first taken over as student council president, he had been easily distracted, to the extent that Laetitia had even wondered whether he was up to the job. Now, however, he seemed to have grown more worthy of the chair.

"All right. Yes, I've been looking out for her ever since she entered the school, and I probably do know her better that anyone else."

Her earliest memory of Percival was her worn-out face the first time they met. At a glance, Laetitia could tell that her heart was badly frayed, her emotions repressed—that she had, in short, been living a life of regret.

It was little wonder. According to the data, she had worked under

Dirk Eberwein, the Institute's so-called Tyrant. She seemed to blame herself for having survived when her fellow designer children hadn't.

And that was precisely why Gallardworth had purchased her as a candidate to wield the Holy Grail.

"Did Gardner ever unlock the Holy Grail's second form?"

"Good heavens, no." Laetitia brushed that insane question aside. "You've read the data on the Holy Grail—on the Amalthean Goat—haven't you? Its second form, the Holy Lance, is only theoretical."

"…Yes, that's true."

The Holy Grail was a powerful Orga Lux, but it was also an incredibly difficult one to wield. Only those who harbored a particularly keen sense of guilt could establish a high compatibility rating with it, and its cost was that the bearer must continue to suffer the burden of atonement. Only those strong enough to do so could wield its soul-robbing light.

"In theory, if one's compatibility rating exceeds ninety-eight percent, it should be possible to activate the Holy Lance. But no one could possibly endure that much guilt."

"Endure, you say?"

"Guilt involves inflicting self-punishment. And what do people do when their guilt becomes too much to bear? They choose suicide."

"…!"

Atonement, when you got down to it, was a matter of personal subjectivity. Social guilt could be settled through punishment, and objectively, if a victim offered their forgiveness, the matter would be settled, whether or not the person responsible forgave themselves. Some were capable of forgetting their sins without atoning, and there were those who were simply unaware of their sins to begin with. And then there were those who continued to blame themselves even when others decided to let go.

Only the latter such group could wield the Holy Grail, and that was precisely why the Holy Lance remained forever out of reach. Before their guilt grew to the point that they could achieve a 98 percent compatibility rating with the Orga Lux, they would seek to atone through their own death.

"In its Holy Lance form, the Amalthean Goat seems to have extraordinary power output, even compared to other first-rate Orga Luxes. But that means that the price exacted by the Holy Lance is that much heavier," Laetitia explained.

"The Holy Lance's abilities, its Light of Judgment... They're an inversion of the Holy Grail's abilities, resulting in extremely potent destructive power, no?" Elliot asked.

"Yes. The Holy Grail manifests for those who seek atonement, while the Holy Lance is for those who want judgment... And the more someone uses the Holy Lance, the more guilt they take on. According to some estimates, using the power of the Holy Lance even once will increase the user's feelings of guilt so much that they would be willing to bite off their own tongue to seek death on the spot."

In other words, the price of using the Holy Lance was nothing short of death itself.

It was no wonder it was so powerful, seeing as it came at such a high price.

But, of course, that was ignoring the fact that there would never be a suitable user in the first place.

Elliot fell silent, sinking deep into thought.

"What's wrong?" Laetitia asked.

When finally he looked up, his expression was strained. "In that case...what if it was possible for an external force to suppress those suicidal thoughts?"

"Like the reconditioning programs used by the foundations? Impossible." Laetitia found the very idea vaguely amusing. "The mind can't just be remodeled like that. And even if it could be, the only thing it would achieve would be to diminish the sense of guilt. There would be no point."

Reducing one's guilt would indeed keep a subject's suicidal thoughts at bay, but then they wouldn't be able to wield the Holy Lance.

Suppressing only someone's suicidal thoughts while maintaining their feelings of guilt would be impossible even for a Genestella with a mental interference or brainwashing ability.

The only exception might be to use an Orga Lux with a particularly high level of power output.

It would, however, be absolute hell for the subject.

After all, they would be constantly tormented, weighed down by immeasurable guilt yet unable to atone for it through death.

"Yes, I see... My apologies, I suppose that was a strange question," Elliot said as he rose to his feet. "Thank you. You've been very helpful. We'll find Gardner, I assure you."

"...I was against letting her have the Holy Grail, you know?" Laetitia murmured despite herself.

Even without reaching its second Holy Lance form, the Holy Grail still put its user through considerable hardship. Percival might have accepted it willingly, but it should never have been placed in the hands of someone as frayed as she was.

"Well, I couldn't go against the wishes of our superiors, and it wasn't up to me."

Nevertheless, Percival had worked hard as a member of Gallardworth's student council, and during her days as a member of Team Lancelot, she had grown brighter, more human even, than when she had first been brought to the school. At least that was how she had seemed to Laetitia.

Taking a sip of her cold tea, she let out a deep sigh. "I wonder where she is now...?"

*

"G-gah...!"

When Kirin shook her head and opened her eyes, she found herself surrounded by collapsed rubble.

She must have lost consciousness, if only for a brief moment.

Right...I tried to block the light with the Fudaraku...

Judging that she would be unable to avoid the onslaught, she had tried cutting through it with the Fudaraku, similar to what Ayato had done earlier. She had managed to avoid a direct hit, but the force of its power had overwhelmed her, the impact throwing her through the wall. Then—

"...!"

She leaped to her feet out of the rubble, just as Percival came tearing toward her through the darkness, a sharp thrust piercing the spot where she had been lying just moments ago.

"So...you're still...alive...?"

As Percival turned her gaze toward Kirin, her head swiveling like a broken doll, her eyes seemed even more vacant than before.

Kirin's first move was to leap from the hole the Holy Lance's attack had gouged through the earth and return to the hall.

At the same time, she checked herself over for damage. A few of her ribs seemed to be broken, but her limbs were unharmed. She was covered in cuts and bruises, but thankfully, none of them seemed particularly deep.

She could keep on fighting.

"...Okay!"

She had yet to come up with a strategy for dealing with that torrent of light, but she hadn't lost yet, and even if she couldn't hope to win, she wasn't about to give up anytime soon.

With that thought, she held the Fudaraku ready in front of her and waited for Percival to emerge from the hole in the ground.

"Y-you're stubborn...aren't you...?" Her foe fixed her in those dull, jet-black eyes as she drew the Holy Lance yet again.

Another flood of light began to build up around it.

Naturally. If she could activate that technique without needing to recharge, there was no reason to hold back.

"Rise...O Light...of Judgment..."

The best thing here would be to dodge it... But at this rate, I'll be dodging forever... In that case...!

Kirin lowered herself to the ground, waiting for the blow to come.

Last time, she had been caught unawares due to making a split-second decision.

This time, she would accept the strike head-on.

She would adopt an altogether different attitude.

"Holy Lance—fire…!"

Golden light overflowed from the Orga Lux, rushing toward her in a mighty torrent.

"Hyaaaaarrrrrgggggghhhhh!"

Letting out a spirited cry, Kirin brought the Fudaraku crashing down, its tip letting off a silver glow as it suppressed the oncoming barrage of light. The blade trembled, her arms supporting it buckled under the pressure, her legs were close to crumbling beneath her.

Power competing against power.

A brilliant flash erupted as gold and silver intercepted each other, neither fighter falling back, when—

"Kyargh!"

The wave of golden light dissipated as the Fudaraku swept downward.

I did it…!

Kirin and the Fudaraku had won in terms of raw power, and yet—

"I'll…take that…"

"Uh-oh!"

By the time the light had faded, Percival was already directly in front of her.

Her basic strategy remained the same—to create a favorable situation using the Holy Lance, then to finish her off in close combat once an opportunity presented itself… Kirin should have realized that.

She wouldn't be able to parry with the Fudaraku in time.

She quickly twisted her body in an attempt to evade, but Percival, as though having foreseen her movements, unleashed not a stabbing thrust, but a sideways slash.

The strike cut from her right shoulder all the way to her left flank, sending blood spurting out. Kirin staggered, mustering all her strength to leap backward and escape Percival's pursuit.

"U-ugh...!"

That blow would have been fatal to any regular person, and even a Genestella would quickly succumb to blood loss. She probably had less than five minutes left of adequate mobility.

Percival, staring at her without expression, readied the Holy Lance—and pulled her right hand behind her back once more.

She never falters...

Kirin doubted she would be able to withstand that deluge of light in her current state.

But just as she thought it was all over, she suddenly realized something.

"S-swell...O Light...o-of Judgment..."

Though Percival's face remained as stolid as ever, a solitary tear spilled from the depths of her cold, black eyes.

"...!"

At that moment, Kirin felt unprecedented rage explode inside of her.

Why hadn't she noticed it sooner?

Percival had been suffering all this time.

Beneath that cold, expressionless exterior, for what must have felt like an eternity.

Not once had she seemed to be fighting through her own volition.

She should have noticed, Kirin berated herself. Ayato would have seen it immediately.

She was furious now, not only at those who had made Percival this way, but at herself for having overlooked it.

She clenched her jaw, ashamed of her own incompetence.

And then—she made up her mind.

"Holy Lance...fire!"

A fresh torrent of light burst forth.

But Kirin had already leaped into the air. Not upward, but to the side—to the wall.

The deluge chased after her as she ran in an arc across the hall, leaping from wall to ceiling, and from there, directly behind Percival's back.

"Here I come!"

Bringing the Fudaraku down with all her strength, she stumbled forward to overpower her foe, who was already preparing to parry with the Holy Lance.

Kirin pressed forward, slashing from top to bottom, but Percival was no average opponent—she responded at once and parried the blade.

She was a formidable foe, a fighter worthy of the deepest respect.

Which was precisely why Kirin couldn't forgive those who had done this to her.

She had fought against so many powerful enemies over the past few years. Ayato, Ardy, Xiaohui—even despicable individuals like Gustave Malraux and the sorcerer who had kidnapped Flora.

But this was the first time she had ever found herself so incensed, so full of rage.

This was an affront to basic human dignity.

"Hyaaaaarrrrrgggggghhhhh!"

Kirin's attacks continued to build up speed.

Yet even then, Percival was still able to take the brunt of her onslaught.

So what next?

Clutching the Fudaraku in the one hand, Kirin unsheathed the Hiinamaru with the other.

The Hiinamaru in her left hand, the Fudaraku in her right.

The Toudou style of swordsmanship didn't specialize in dual-wielding techniques. This was something she had developed herself.

Back when she had fought against Gustave's Spartoi, she had merely been making up for the difference in numbers—this time was different.

The Hiinamaru let out a flash of light, while the Fudaraku danced through the air.

Little by little, she began to push Percival back.

She hadn't been intentionally holding back before this. The reason she hadn't attempted to use both swords was that she didn't know whether the Hiinamaru would be able to withstand a blow from the Holy Lance. It may have been the ancient swordsmith Kunikane Youkei's greatest work, but it was still ultimately just a regular Japanese sword. If it collided directly with an Orga Lux of that power, it wouldn't be at all surprising if it shattered then and there. Should that happen, Kirin would find herself speared by the Holy Lance before she could so much as blink.

But there was no point worrying about that now.

If she didn't give this fight her absolute best, she wouldn't stand a chance of beating Percival.

As her repertoire of abilities and skills collided violently with the Holy Lance, Kirin's strength ebbed, and she felt the impacts of the blows wash over her.

The words of Ayato's father Masatsugu sounded in the back of her head: *"The key lies in precision, in how thoroughly you can put yourself into one swing of the sword."*

"R-right...!"

Taking her flurry of techniques to the next level, the flash of Kirin's swords increased in intensity yet again.

From the Yatsuhashi to the Kanae, from the Kakitsubata to the Sekirei—

Percival was on the defensive now, unable to launch into her own counterattack.

At first glance, Kirin's combination of moves might have resembled her Conjoined Cranes technique—but this was something different.

Given Percival's perceptive eyes, the Conjoined Cranes would be ineffective here.

After all, the technique was based on analyzing the minutia of one's opponent's breathing, timing, and gaze to block their attacks and push them into a corner.

As such, while she was linking various disparate sword forms as she did in the Conjoined Cranes, this wasn't that technique per se. It wasn't even her New Conjoined Cranes.

If she had to give it a name, she would probably go with Senba-zuru, in honor of her beloved old sword.

Now her every strike was delivered with her full body as she poured her strength into each swing and thrust. The Conjoined Cranes was a series of endless and unceasing attacks akin to the folding of an origami crane—and this was even faster.

Under regular circumstances, she wouldn't be able to continue pouring her energy into a combination like this.

Right now, however, she had been pushed far past her limit.

"Ah, haah... Aaaaahhhhh...!" Percival howled beneath her expressionless exterior.

With the Hiinamaru, Kirin kept the Holy Lance in check, while she used the Fudaraku to repel it.

The Holy Lance—the Amalthean Goat—spun through the air, its blade swirling and dancing as the Fudaraku and the Hiinamaru crossed blades and slashed into Percival's chest, slicing open a cross shape.

Just as the Amalthean Goat pierced the ground, Percival fell to the floor in a heap.

The wound had nearly been fatal. Kirin's foe may have sought death, but still it eluded her.

Percival's wounds were probably around the same depth as Kirin's own, perhaps a little deeper. She wouldn't be able to move anymore.

Though, of course, the same was true for Kirin.

"Phew..."

Exhaling weakly, she felt her knees quiver.

Her senses were already fading.

"I'm sorry, everyone... The rest...is up to you..."

With those faint words, she collapsed by Percival's side, her consciousness sinking into darkness.

CHAPTER 7
SHOWDOWN WITH THE VARDA-VAOS

The fortieth floor of Hotel Elnath, the highest point accessible by the building's regular elevators, was occupied by a club lounge.

No sooner did Sylvia and the others step out from the elevator than they headed down the corridor, lightly brushing aside the lounge staff offering up reverent greetings.

At the end of the passageway was a door, needlessly extravagant, that opened with a heavy rumbling when Sylvia held out her school crest. Beyond it was a waiting room fitted with a tasteful sofa, and at the wall farther back was another elevator.

This one connected the fortieth floor of the building to the forty-second at the top. The forty-first floor was dedicated to administrative and management offices, so this elevator only served to connect their current floor with the domed aerial garden at the building's zenith.

"U-um... I know we're already here, but is it really okay for me to go inside...?" This question came from Minato Wakamiya, her gaze wandering restlessly as she hid behind Sylvia's back. "I mean, isn't this basically Asterisk's holy sanctuary? I thought only student

council presidents could go inside... Supposedly not even foundation executives are allowed..."

"Oh-ho, it isn't such a big deal. It's only a garden. The Rikka
Garden Summit is just a symbol of student autonomy, that's all,"
Claudia said with a chuckle.

That was certainly true, but it wasn't the whole story. As Claudia
and Sylvia understood all too well, the Rikka Garden Summit was
ultimately a tool for the foundations to avoid criticism. It allowed
them to argue that student affairs were ultimately decided by the
representatives of the students themselves. Of course, there were
some projects submitted to the Rikka Garden Summit by students,
but the vast majority came directly from the foundations via the
student council presidents under their control, who, with very few
exceptions—namely Xinglou—were obligated to follow the instructions of their parent organization.

"I didn't think you would actually come join us, no questions
asked," Claudia said, still half-astonished. "Thank you."

"Of course I came! I already owe you so much!" Minato exclaimed,
clenching her fist in front of her chest.

She apparently hadn't been able to get a ticket to the championship match, and so she had been intending to watch it privately with
her old teammates.

"It's like they say, pity doesn't do anyone any good. You've got to
help people out when you can."

It was true that Sylvia had gone out of her way to help Minato's
friend Chloe in the past, but that was more for her own sake—or
strictly speaking, for Queenvale's.

There was something to be said for helping others out of a sense of
altruism without expecting anything in return, but considering the
circumstances, she was genuinely grateful that Minato had decided
to join them.

"There's something I need to ask you before we go any farther.
Once we're inside, there won't be any turning back. We'll be forced

to fight an incredibly dangerous adversary. Are you really okay with that?" Claudia asked, her expression serious.

"Um... I don't really know what's going on, but this is all to help people, right?" Minato responded, turning to Sylvia.

"Yep, that's right," Sylvia answered. "I've got to do this to save someone I care about and to protect others dear to me."

"Then I'm totally fine with it! I'll come along, wherever you need me!" Minato said with a carefree smile.

"...Thank you, Minato."

She had an honest heart, the kind that never wavered.

The courage to keep on pursuing her dreams without giving up, even after enduring forty-nine consecutive losses in official ranked matches.

Sylvia was beyond grateful.

"I understand," Claudia said. "In that case, I can let you cover my back with peace of mind... Now, it's time. We should go."

Indeed, the championship match was just about to get underway.

The three exchanged measured glances, then stepped into the elevator.

At that very instant, an eerie sense of aversion rose up inside Minato's chest, along with a strong urge to turn around.

"...! U-um, Sylvia...! Is this...?!"

"I...see... So this is the field the Varda-Vaos uses to keep people away...!"

But so long as their wills were resolute, it wasn't intolerable.

Sylvia reached out to the air-window and shut the elevator doors. After a short ascent, they opened once more.

What lay before the group was a familiar sight to the two student council presidents:

Waterways stretched in all directions, while well-maintained garden beds were in full bloom. In the center of it all was a small hill, atop which stood a small arbor, fitted with a hexagonal table modeled after an asterisk. If they had come to attend one of the regular sessions of the Rikka Garden Summit, no doubt Claudia and Sylvia would have gone to take their usual seats.

But their objective this time wasn't a tabletop game of conspiracy and intrigue, but real battle.

"...We know you're here, Varda-Vaos. Why don't you show yourself?" Sylvia called out quietly, her voice nevertheless filled with open hostility.

At that moment, the air ahead of them warped, and the Varda-Vaos—the Orga Lux in control of Ursula Svend's body—emerged.

"Huh?! Wh-where did *she* come from...?!"

"She must have been using another field, like the one meant to keep outsiders from entering. A barrier to interfere with our thoughts so we couldn't see her."

Minato, who had never before witnessed the Varda-Vaos's abilities firsthand, stared back wide-eyed. Sylvia had briefly explained what they would be going up against, but it was only natural that she was taken aback once she encountered it for real.

Of the three of them, only Sylvia had directly confronted this enemy before.

In that respect, it was a little odd that Claudia seemed completely unperturbed.

"I would not have expected anyone to enter this place. And your timing... I see. Yes, you must have realized that we cannot issue Orphelia instructions now. Which means you must be moving against Madiath and Dirk, too, I assume?"

At that, the Varda-Vaos pulled back the hood of the robe shrouding her face, revealing a head of dusky blue hair.

She seemed to have surmised their intentions.

"Sylvia Lyyneheym and the user of the Pan-Dora...Claudia Enfield, I believe your name was? And...hmm, a new face... No, wait. Those vibrations... The Járngreipr? Which would make you Minato Wakamiya." All this the Varda-Vaos muttered to herself while looking them over one by one.

"D-do you know me…?" Minato, who probably hadn't expected to be addressed by name, stared back in surprise.

"Ah, I see," Claudia observed. "So you recognize humans not as individuals, but as users of certain Orga Luxes."

"I can remember your names if necessary, but I find it a little difficult to distinguish between you humans. You are easier to recall when associated with my brethren," the Varda-Vaos responded without any observable artifice. "Now, perhaps I need not ask, but why are you here?"

"To bring an end to your plans, naturally," Sylvia answered as she activated her sword-type Lux, giving it a swing to test its condition.

The Fólkvangr had been rendered unusable during her match against Orphelia, but this spare Lux was a priceless treasure, carefully tuned especially for her.

Claudia likewise pulled out her Pan-Dora, while Minato activated her Járngreipr.

"To stop our plans…? I am afraid that will not be possible."

Far from readying for combat, the Varda-Vaos, on the other hand, continued to speak with little concern.

"I do not know where or how you acquired this information, but our plan is already in motion. Orphelia is merely the final part."

At that moment, a violent explosion erupted in the distance, causing the entire building to sway dangerously.

"Was that…?!"

"Looks like it's started."

Outside the glass walls of the dome, explosions erupted one after another throughout the city of Asterisk, sending flames roiling high into the sky.

No, that wasn't entirely right.

Strictly speaking, they seemed to be concentrated around the city's outer edge.

"What have you done?!"

"The Valiants we deployed have merely begun their operations.

Their main task is to destroy the transportation system and related facilities. So as long as no one interferes, there should be minimal human casualties...for now."

"...You're trying to stop anyone from escaping Asterisk." Claudia glared back, likely having inferred their enemies' reasoning.

Now that she looked carefully, Sylvia could see that most of the damage was around the port block and the airship departure and landing areas.

"You're a swift thinker. Precisely. Some individuals with unique abilities may be able to fly or swim across the lake...but they will be rare exceptions. Most of the humans remaining in Asterisk will be sacrificed to Orphelia."

"I won't let you do that!" Sylvia cried, rushing forward and lashing out at the Varda-Vaos.

"I told you. Stopping us will not be possible." The Varda-Vaos immediately caught the oncoming blow with a huge black battle-ax that materialized in her right hand.

"Ugh...!"

Sylvia had poured her energy into that blow, but her foe hadn't even flinched—rather, she had swept her aside as if she was no more than a fly.

Ursula was her former teacher, and objectively speaking she was indeed exceptionally talented. But Sylvia had grown considerably since they last met and hadn't expected to face such a huge gulf in ability. This, then, could only be the raw power of the Varda-Vaos itself as an Orga Lux.

"Your main ability is mental interference, right? Is that what you're doing?"

She had heard about the power from Ayato, but to think it could be this potent...

"Of course. We are the remnants of God. In our true form, this would be nothing."

"God...? You've got a big head on you there, huh?" Sylvia murmured, on high alert as she kept pace with her foe.

Then—

"I know how you feel, but you shouldn't run off ahead."

"I'll help!"

Claudia and Minato stepped forward to secure her flanks.

"Three against one…? I do not intend to lose, but just in case…" As the Varda-Vaos raised her left hand, the air distorted once more, with several autonomous puppets appearing in the room.

In number, they totaled—

"Around twenty, I'd say," Claudia called.

"Wh-wh-whoa…!" Minato shouted.

She had expected some Valiants, but not this many.

"The three of you are certainly strong—but only according to the standards of this world. From my perspective, you are little more than infants hailing from a primitive plane of existence." The Varda-Vaos's emotionless eyes gleamed, the urm-manadite at her chest letting out an obsidian light.

"M-my head…!" No sooner had that light reached her than Minato fell to her knees, clutching her skull.

"Ugh…!" Claudia similarly backed away, her face contorting in agony.

The black light emitted by the Varda-Vaos directly interfered with its target's psyche, allowing the Orga Lux to falsify memories, control one's consciousness, or even destroy one's mind itself.

"Have you forgotten, Sylvia Lyyneheym? You were once reduced to crawling in the face of my power."

"I…don't need…to hear that from you…!" she gasped, grabbing Minato by the nape of her neck and pulling her away.

The pain in Minato's skull alleviated once she had established enough distance. But the Varda-Vaos's black light currently covered a range of around ten meters, and it was only growing more powerful. The Valiants, moreover, had established a defensive perimeter around their master.

"Perhaps you came in small numbers hoping to avoid detection…? You should have at least brought the wielder of the Ser

Veresta. Though if I wanted, I could contain even one of your Four Colored Runeswords."

The Varda-Vaos's boast was plainspoken, but it was probably true. Sylvia doubted that this one-of-a-kind Orga Lux, with its own ego and the power to usurp its user's body, would see any meaning in elevating itself or denigrating others. As far as the Varda-Vaos was concerned, what she had just said was mere fact.

Still…

"Hah! Ha-ha-ha…!" Sylvia's brow furrowed in response to the pounding inside her head, but even so, she let out a dauntless laugh.

"…Is something amusing?" the Varda-Vaos asked, her voice carrying a hint of suspicion, though her countenance remained unchanged.

"No, it's just… I'm *the* Sigrdrífa, and well, it sounds like you've got a pretty low opinion of me…!" Sylvia responded in challenge. "Sure…us Stregas might be no match for an Orga Lux… But you know… There *was* once a Strega strong enough to upend all of Asterisk…! Even you have to know that…! I mean, she was Madiath Mesa's—Lamina Mortis's—own tag partner…!"

"…What…?"

Sylvia herself had only recently learned about her, when Helga had provided her with data on the Festa as they searched for clues on the Golden Bough Alliance.

She was referring to the Strega Akari Yachigusa, who alongside Madiath Mesa had once triumphed in the Phoenix.

But while she had won the Festa, it was Madiath who had confronted their opponents in every match, so there was little record of her achievements in battle. Yet while they had fought together in the Festa only once, her abilities as a Strega were plain to see.

In short, her overall strength was so shocking that even though she had never before entered the rankings, those who witnessed her performance in the Festa granted her an unofficial title— the Witch of Magnificent Ice, Fimbulvetr.

"And you know what *my* ability is, right…? The power to evoke all kinds of phenomena through music…?"

"…No…!"

Sylvia took a deep breath and burst into song, her voice bombastic and sonorous.

"Come ye, O three winters, freeze ye the forest of all that dwells betwixt heaven and earth."

At that moment, the movement of mana around her began to slow.

Fimbulvetr's extraordinary ability was the power to completely halt the flow of mana within its effective area, negating not only the powers of Dantes and Stregas, but also all Luxes and Orga Luxes that relied on the conversion of mana to function. Naturally, without an energy source, those devices would simply stop functioning.

Though Sylvia's ability was remarkably versatile, the amount of prana it required depended on the difficulty of the task at hand. If she tried to imitate Fimbulvetr's powers in full, she would exhaust her prana reserves in a matter of seconds. Not only that, since the effects of her songs grew in potency the longer she sang, the field would likewise cease expanding when she stopped. In short, the area would be too narrow, the duration too short.

"O winter of wind summon ye time; O winter of the sword call ye action; O winter of the wolf invite ye slumber."

Given the limits of her abilities, Sylvia focused not on freezing the mana around her but on slowing its movements to a crawl.

"No…!"

For the first time, the Varda-Vaos's expression was one of dismay.

Sylvia's plan was working.

The black light on the verge of consuming the aerial garden drew back at the edges, the conversion of mana unable to keep up. This wasn't the kind of problem that could be resolved by increasing one's power output.

"Dull, rust, grow ye stagnant, and silence all life, O winters three!"

At last, the movement of mana around them had been reduced to around one-tenth its usual level.

"Sylvia, leave the Valiants to us," Claudia declared.

"Go, Sylvia!" Minato yelled.

With that, her two companions headed off in separate directions and made for the Valiants surrounding the Varda-Vaos. The autonomous puppets were unusually lethargic as they moved to intercept—little surprise seeing as they were powered by manadite. There was bound to be a drop in energy under these circumstances.

Claudia's Pan-Dora and Minato's Járngreipr would likewise be largely inoperable, but given their respective skill levels, they ought to be able to prevail against the Valiants even outnumbered.

With the Valiants under control, the only one left was—

"...Stop, Sylvia Lyyneheym!"

In stark contrast to her previous attitude, the Varda-Vaos lunged toward Sylvia in a sideward swipe, her eyes blazing.

Nonetheless, the battle-ax in her right hand had now shrunk to less than half its original size, and although the blow was a hard one, it no longer overwhelmed her immediately. It seemed the Varda-Vaos's own power output had similarly fallen.

"You're showing some pretty *human* emotions there...!" Sylvia, having finished her song, quipped as she pushed forward.

The Varda-Vaos clicked her tongue and fell back. "Inadvertently, yes. Surrounded by human emotions for so long, I suppose it was inevitable."

"Oh? So you're letting *people* influence you?"

Sylvia stepped to one side, feinted, then lashed out with an attack directed to the right side of her foe's body—which the Varda-Vaos promptly caught with a new jet-black ax emanating from her left hand. Her opponent was now wielding two weapons, but as she couldn't draw on a large amount of power, that required diverting resources from elsewhere.

"Adaptation, not influence. And as I said, inadvertent!"

Sylvia stood her ground as she parried fresh blows from every possible angle.

Her foe was faster than she remembered, but her overall technique remained familiar.

She parried the ax barreling toward her right side with her sword, then stepped in toward the blow aimed at her left, closing in and using her elbow to hold back the Varda-Vaos's arm. The blade of black light grazed against her shoulder, but she paid that no mind as she slammed her knee into the Varda-Vaos's gut with all her might.

"Gah…!"

Having thrown her foe backward, Sylvia launched into a fresh pursuit, but the Varda-Vaos adjusted her fighting posture and threw both axes forward to keep her opponent in check. Of course, Sylvia could easily repel those weapons, and with her foe now unarmed, she had just been handed an easy opportunity to—

"…!"

As she waited for the right timing, she was suddenly hit by two counterblows—sharp jabs from the sides of her foe's hands. The strikes dug into her cheeks and side, but thankfully, the wounds weren't too deep.

Once more, she fell back to establish some distance between herself and the Varda-Vaos.

"Right, right. Ursula had a first-class physique… It wasn't like I'd forgotten, but it didn't occur to me that you'd use it for yourself."

"Good grief…" The Varda-Vaos manifested a fresh black ax in her hands, albeit at an unusually slow speed. "It's like fighting without being able to breathe. You're a shrewd one, I'll give you that."

"If you had bothered to watch my quarterfinal fight with Orphelia, you'd have seen I'm pretty good at countering people's abilities. Especially when it comes to enemies who've already beaten me once before."

Slowing down the movement of the surrounding mana looked to be even more effective than she had hoped.

However, the song's effect wouldn't last much longer.

Of course, she could try singing it again, but there would inevitably be a lag, and something told her the Varda-Vaos wouldn't hesitate to capitalize on that.

"Hmm... And this from someone who failed abysmally at stopping Orphelia?"

"Ha, can't say that doesn't sting...!"

Her only choice here was to follow through quickly and decide this bout while she still had the advantage.

And so, holding her sword down low, she closed the gap with her opponent and slashed upward with all her strength.

"Tch...!"

The Varda-Vaos crossed her two axes to block the attack, but Sylvia instead launched a sharp thrust to her abdomen where she had lowered her guard. Her foe at once brought her right hand back to block it with only moments to spare, and Sylvia followed with an uninterrupted and exquisitely precise chain of strikes.

Overall, Sylvia's close-combat abilities were clearly the superior of the two. At this rate, she should be able to push through.

"...You attack with determination...!" the Varda-Vaos growled, now on the defensive. "But I wonder... Does this human body not belong to someone precious to you?"

"Huh...?"

The moment that she heard those words, Sylvia felt something snap inside her.

"Ugggggghhhhh!"

The Varda-Vaos managed to block Sylvia's full-powered swipe, but the impact sent her flying backward before rolling across the floor into a flower bed.

"You're going to try taking her hostage *now*?" Sylvia, suppressing her rage, slowly closed the distance between them. "Don't you dare insult me. Do you think my resolve is that weak, after all this time? I won't hesitate again. I'll even cut off one or two of your limbs if I have to. Fortunately, there are some good healers in this city, so we'll be able to reconnect them if necessary."

The Varda-Vaos rose unsteadily to her feet, readying her axes.

"If Ursula ends up hating or resenting me, I can live with that. I'll do my best to apologize and make amends, but I'm fine if she doesn't forgive me. I just want her back. That's all."

"...I see. I suppose I still don't understand you humans!" With that, the Varda-Vaos suddenly launched an attack.

Sylvia easily dodged the strike, slipping through her foe's guard and cutting at her legs.

"...!"

As the Varda-Vaos fell to the ground without so much as a grunt, Sylvia plunged her blade of light toward her.

Even if the Orga Lux itself was undamaged, it relied on the human body it had usurped to move, so escape would prove impossible if it couldn't physically move that body's legs. What's more, the Varda-Vaos still had only limited access to her own abilities.

Now, at long last—

"...You've let down your guard, haven't you?"

"...?!"

At that moment, the Varda-Vaos's urm-manadite began to glow with jet-black light.

The light, much weaker than before, was still enough to cause a strong headache—but at the same time, it offered Sylvia the smallest of openings.

However—

"I only needed a moment. At this distance, in this position, even the briefest window of opportunity is enough for me to do this..."

The next second, the Varda-Vaos's own body—that oversized mechanical necklace, disproportionately large around Ursula's neck—wriggled as if it was alive, extending a tentacle-like cord to entangle Sylvia.

Then, as the urm-manadite in its center glowed ominously, her consciousness was abruptly cut off.

*

Just as Minato dispatched her eighth Valiant, she felt the flow of mana in the air around her returning to normal.

"Uh-oh…"

Peering deeper into the garden, she spotted the woman with dusky blue hair lying sprawled on the ground while Sylvia loomed over her.

That probably meant Sylvia had won. From Minato's vantage point, Sylvia had dominated her opponent from start to finish. She truly was Queenvale's one and only Sigrdrífa.

"Hey, Sylvia," she called out—only to freeze when she took in her face.

Her expression was the coldest and most inorganic Minato had ever seen.

"Huh…?"

A horrifying sense of foreboding took root in her brain.

"Enfield! I'm sorry, but I'll need you to take care of the rest of them!"

With that, she blasted away two more Valiants, leaving the rest to Claudia as she bolted across the garden.

"W-Wakamiya…?! Wait, please…!" Claudia called out behind her, urging restraint.

But Minato's body was by now practically moving of its own accord.

"Sylvia!"

"…"

Yet as Minato approached, Sylvia remained completely silent.

Around her chest hung the necklace previously worn by the woman now lying prone on the ground.

Minato had promised to help after agreeing not to delve too deep into the present situation, but she had been informed of the true nature of their opponent—a mind-controlling Orga Lux with the ability to usurp its user's body.

It couldn't be…

"This is an unexpected discovery."

That murmur was clearly spoken with Sylvia's beautiful voice.

But something was different.

Minato couldn't quite put her finger on it, but something was *definitely* different.

"I only took over this human to make my escape, but with this level of compatibility… And to think, a Strega, too…"

Sylvia, flexing her right hand several times, retrieved the sword-type Lux that had fallen to the ground. "Excellent timing. Minato Wakamiya, why don't you keep me company while I acclimate to this new vessel?"

"…!"

Sylvia's sword flashed through the air, a dazzling strike careening toward her.

Minato repelled the blow with her Járngreipr, then leaped backward to establish some distance as she glowered at Sylvia—or rather, at the Orga Lux.

"You aren't… You aren't really Sylvia, are you…?!"

"Indeed. I am Varda-Vaos. As leader of my abandoned brethren, I shall prepare this world for what is to come."

With those words, the Varda-Vaos launched into a flurry of ferocious attacks. Two attacks in quick succession from above, before her sword arced gracefully to the left in a sideswipe, then to the right in a reverse diagonal cut from waist to shoulder—all with the intent of taking Minato's life.

She's too close…! I need to fall back…!

Minato had never before fought directly against Sylvia—but she was well aware just how fierce Queenvale's number one was in battle.

Minato, at the time still young and immature, had first met Sylvia more than two years ago, and the other girl had quickly become a close friend and benefactor. If not for Sylvia's intervention, Minato doubted she would have ever developed the relationships she had now.

But, of course, she too had grown considerably stronger. She had pulled through her rigorous training with Xinglou at the Liangshan and now wielded a powerful weapon of her own, the Járngreipr. She may have dropped out of the Lindvolus, but she had made it all the way to fighting Ayato Amagiri himself.

"So I'm not about to just give up…!"

Minato eluded a swing directed straight for her neck and then, twisting around her foe, delivered a powerful backhand chop to her chest.

Genkuu style—*Spiral Rend.*

"Umph."

Her fist, carrying immense force thanks to the Járngreipr equipped to it, blasted the Varda-Vaos backward. Her foe, however, successfully guarded herself against damage. It should have been a considerable blow, but the Varda-Vaos's expression remained undeterred.

"Ah, yes, the Járngreipr's ability is mass conversion. You've mastered it well. Not bad at all."

"I'm not looking for praise…!"

Minato closed the distance once more by approaching from her flank, spinning around as she unleashed another punch.

Genkuu style—*Spiral Rend.*

However, the Varda-Vaos easily dodged the blow by tilting her body half to one side. Minato followed through with a backward kick and an elbow strike, but she was unable to make contact.

As though anticipating her attacks, the Varda-Vaos had dodged them all.

"…I thought as much," the Orga Lux murmured, easily countering Minato's palm strike.

"Ugh…!"

Her left arm was sliced open, and she fell back grimacing in pain.

The wound was a deep one. It was bleeding heavily, and she could barely move her arm.

"Minato Wakamiya. Have you been aiming only for my own body?"

"…!"

The Varda-Vaos had hit the mark.

Even if the Orga Lux had hijacked it, that body belonged to Sylvia. She couldn't risk harming her, too.

"Don't feel ashamed. From what I've learned, what you are experiencing is a natural state for humans. Rather, it was this Sylvia Lyyneheym, with her utter lack of hesitation, who was the anomaly."

If Minato wasn't mistaken, there was a hint of satisfaction in the Varda-Vaos's voice.

"Yes. That is fine. You humans are simply like that. Acting only in accordance with your thoughts, in obeisance to your desires. Yes, it's only normal for your kind."

"Shut up! We're not dolls for you to play with!" Minato cried back.

The Varda-Vaos, however, appeared not to have heard her. "Now then, what shall I try next…?"

She took a deep breath, then—

"Let's tear down our walls! Let's surpass ourselves! No begrudging our wounds, run, run!"

An easily recognizable song began to spill from her lips.

That was Sylvia's go-to song for boosting her physical abilities.

Minato watched as mana began to swirl violently around her foe.

"You've even taken her singing powers…?!"

Taken aback by what she was seeing, she let go of her wound and readied another punch.

If the Orga Lux could even use Sylvia's abilities, then—

Still singing, the Varda-Vaos took off at a run—her speed much faster than it had been a moment before.

Then, lashing out with divine speed, she aimed straight for Minato's heart.

"Ugh…!"

It was only thanks to the weight of the Járngreipr that she managed to block it. But how was she to continue fighting one-handed?

And the Varda-Vaos wasn't finished.

"If thoughts alone can't reach you, if wishes alone aren't enough, then I'll go beyond my limits. I'll keep pushing on!"

"Don't you... Don't you sing that song!"

Minato repelled the Varda-Vaos's blade with her Járngreipr and lashed out with a sideward kick to knock her opponent's legs out from under her.

Genkuu style—*Sickle Ring.*

While she didn't manage to make contact, her foe, perhaps not having expected her previous move, fell back.

"That song belongs to Sylvia!"

Minato knew even without being explicitly told just how important that song was to Sylvia. *Anyone* who had heard it would be able to understand that.

Though it had the same words, and though it was being sung in the same voice, the Varda-Vaos's version was somehow different— the encouragement, the cheer, the warmth that normally imbued the melody was hollow and empty.

"What? A song is a song. There's no difference so long as you have the proper technique and tune... Like this."

With that, the Orga Lux interrupted her ability-boosting melody to shift into another.

"Rejoice, rejoice at our heroes' triumphant return, for the silver gleaming gates of war now stand before us!"

I know this one...!

It was a brave, soul-inspiring battle cry.

The mana began to swirl around them, more shadowy figures than the eye could count appearing behind the Varda-Vaos's back— faceless women with wings outstretched and swords raised.

It was the song that Sylvia had used against Orphelia in the deciding match of the last Lindvolus, summoning up a legion of Valkyries modeled after herself. Minato remembered watching the live broadcast with her eyes glued to the air-window.

"The heavens my guide, my sword my prayer, my wishes my blade as I sing this grand song aloud!"

At that moment, more than a dozen Valkyrie maidens attacked Minato all at once.

"That's enough…!"

With her Járngreipr, she repelled the blades of light careening toward her from all directions, knocking down the Valkyries, kicking them away, and getting the better of them—but still she was hopelessly outnumbered. The blows she failed to defend against viciously struck her arms and legs.

"Hah…! Hah…! U-ugh…!"

The song's effect eventually wore off and the warrior maidens vanished, leaving Minato with lacerations all over her body.

She was barely able to stand. It was only thanks to her experiences fighting against numerous opponents in the Gryps that she hadn't sustained a fatal injury.

"Hmm. Perhaps that will do to verify this Strega's abilities. In that case…"

Casting her sword-type Lux to one side, the Varda-Vaos unleashed a torrent of jet-black light straight for Minato.

"Ugh…! Aaaaahhhhh!"

Her skull pounding like something was rampaging inside her head, she collapsed to the floor.

"Good. My power is at its fullest. Wonderful. I've never had a body like this before," the Varda-Vaos murmured with satisfaction.

Then, no longer interested in drawing out their fight, she gave the black ax in her hand one final swing.

Just before it could cleave through Minato's neck—

"Mwah?"

A blade of light carved through the air and struck out at the Varda-Vaos.

The Orga Lux repelled it effortlessly, but with her attention diverted, the glow of black light faded slightly.

"Geez... This is why I told you to wait."

Minato felt her body being whisked through the air. Before she knew it, Claudia was clutching her in her arms.

"...Claudia Enfield?"

The Orga Lux appeared on guard as she braced herself with her ax, but Claudia swiftly darted out of range of the black light. Then, the radiant blade that the Varda-Vaos had repelled—one-half of Claudia's Pan-Dora—spun through the air before falling safely back into its user's hand.

The whole thing had proceeded as though Claudia had foreseen every moment.

"Thanks to you heading off on your own, it took a little while to clean up the Valiants. I actually meant to finish them off sooner, you know?"

Glancing around, it looked like the Valiants had indeed been destroyed.

"Are you okay? There's still a task that only you can carry out, Miss Wakamiya, so please, keep to the sidelines for now," Claudia said as though admonishing a child, before letting Minato fall to the ground with a thud.

"Something only I can do...? N-no, you don't mean to fight her alone? We should at least fight together...!"

Minato, who had just a few minutes ago rushed into battle despite Claudia's protestations, had no right to object. Even so, with the Varda-Vaos now in control of Sylvia's abilities, their foe was an extraordinary threat. While she wasn't sure how useful she would be in the fight, Minato could at least act as a decoy if push came to shove.

"Don't be silly. Look at you. You needn't worry. I'll handle her by myself," Claudia reassured Minato easily, as she tried to push herself up from the floor.

"Huh…?"

"You might not know this, but I'm actually pretty strong." Claudia beamed as Minato stared up at her.

Of course, Minato was well aware that Claudia was one of the most powerful students at Seidoukan Academy—she was the student council president, and the school's second highest-ranked fighter with the alias Parca Morta. On top of that, she wielded the Pan-Dora, an incredibly powerful Orga Lux with the ability to predict the future, and she had led her team to victory in the previous Gryps tournament. She was one of the strongest individuals not just at Seidoukan, but in Asterisk as a whole.

All the same, from what Minato could see, not even *she* was skilled enough to take on the Varda-Vaos in Sylvia's body by herself.

"Minato Wakamiya is right, Claudia Enfield," the Varda-Vaos declared plainly. "You are strong, but still not as strong as Sylvia Lyyneheym. I have her powers at my disposal, along with my own. There is no way you can defeat me alone. Even using the Pan-Dora's clairvoyance."

She presented this information as indisputable fact.

"Oh-ho. Why, thank you for the advice. By the way, may I ask you a question?" Claudia responded while keeping her distance.

"…What?"

"About your goals, the Golden Bough Alliance's. You intend to take the lives of everyone here in Asterisk using Erenshkigal's abilities. We already know that."

"…?!"

Minato's eyes bulged as she froze in terror at the sheer ridiculousness of Claudia's claim.

She had known that *something* was going on…but to think that the situation was one of life or death…

"But that must only be a means to an end, I assume? What we don't know is your purpose beyond that," Claudia continued.

The Varda-Vaos fell silent for a moment before slowly responding.

"Very well. Even knowing, it will be too late for you to do anything about it... For *anyone* to do anything about it." She paused there, glancing up at the sky—the cloud-covered firmament beyond the glass ceiling. "Do you know what mana *is*? What *we* are...? I didn't think so. We are the abandoned."

"...The abandoned?"

"Yes. Of the world you humans call *the other side*, a universe filled with mana, a plane of existence where gods exist. Mana is, so to speak, the breath of the gods. You humans are constantly drawing in oxygen and exhaling carbon dioxide, no? In the same way, mana is produced through our mere existence."

The Varda-Vaos's voice sounded almost nostalgic.

"Mana is an incredibly useful element, as I'm sure even you humans realize, given how much you use it. But it has its limits. Living things cannot sustain themselves in places where its concentration is too high. Unlike the barren, death-ridden universe on *this* side, *ours* is overflowing with mana."

Beyond the dome, the sound of explosions continued intermittently. Even now, a disaster was beginning to unfold.

Nonetheless, Minato found herself absorbed by the Varda-Vaos's words.

"The stronger the god's powers, the more mana it produces. And the most powerful entity on the other side is our chief god, residing in our sun. Our chief god has lain dormant for ages, but he continues to produce enormous quantities of mana. And so, the closer a planet is to the sun, the higher the concentration of mana. Our Mercury is no longer an environment suitable to life."

"There was life on Mercury...?" Claudia asked in astonishment.

"I told you. The universe on the other side is abundant in mana. Each celestial body is inhabited by its own god, whose power is immense within their own planetary sphere. Those gods seek and protect the creatures that believe in them. Well, they do occasionally punish their subjects on a whim, but in general, they take the side of the life-forms within their domain. So all the planets on the other side are inhabited by human life. Or should I say, *were* inhabited. Now even our Venus is in danger."

For the first time, the Varda-Vaos's expression clouded over.

"...The god of our Earth has taken certain countermeasures to protect the humans of their own planet: disposing of excess mana when it becomes too much to bear. They send it to a different world in a different universe—that is, *here*. Your world is a dumping ground for our surplus mana."

"What...? So if mana keeps growing in abundance here, you're saying everyone will die...?" Minato murmured under her breath.

"That's right. It may take millions, perhaps even tens of millions of years, but yes... No matter how immeasurable a god's powers, it isn't easy to break through the walls of the universe. But we found a way—by transferring huge quantities of meteorites. You know what I'm talking about, don't you?"

"The Invertia?" Claudia whispered softly.

The Varda-Vaos nodded coolly. "The *hole* was bored by the Invertia. Even now, mana continues to flow from the other side to this one. And we, urm-manadite, are the crystallization of that mana. We are remnants of the gods themselves, so if our purity level is high enough, we can exercise our own free will. In the past, there were others like me—my brethren who could act alone without the help of any human—but not anymore. That is why I must lead. Why *I* must open the way."

"...Open the way to what?" Claudia asked quietly.

With a sniff, the Varda-Vaos spread her hands. "To make this world more suitable for us to live and operate in. We cannot return to the other side. Even if we could, we don't belong there anymore. We were abandoned. So our only option is to reshape *this* world. Wouldn't you agree?"

"What are you saying...?!" Minato whispered.

Wasn't that practically an invasion?

"Don't misunderstand me. Our hope is for coexistence. With you—with Genestella."

"Considering what you're proposing, that's hard to believe…"

"It's true. There are almost no other urm-manadite crystals that can operate independently as I can. Most of my brethren cannot function without the aid of a human and an exterior mechanism. They need users."

Claudia pondered this for a moment, her expression serious. "When you say *coexistence*, you're only talking about Genestella, aren't you?"

"That's right. Regular humans—*old* humans—are unnecessary. Harmful, even. They and their integrated enterprise foundations will never accept us."

"I see. I understand your goal, I think… Your purpose."

"Oh? Then pray tell," the Varda-Vaos prodded.

Claudia looked her squarely in the eye before answering, "You're trying to sow discord between ordinary people and Genestella. You're trying to bring about a conflict so huge that there will be no turning back."

"What…?!"

Minato was left stunned by this suggestion. It surpassed even her wildest imagination.

"The characterization is wrong, but in general terms, yes," the Varda-Vaos agreed. "I hope to usher in a world ruled by Genestella."

"The characterization is wrong?" Claudia repeated.

"From our point of view, we will be liberating Genestella like yourself from the oppression of ordinary humans."

As condescending as that declaration was, the Varda-Vaos seemed to honestly believe it.

"We have no need of your help, but I'm sure that means nothing to you. I understand now, why this child never showed me so much as a glimpse of this in any of my nightmares. As an Orga Lux, she *wants* that world you're striving to create. You didn't want to get in the way now, did you?" she asked, fixing her own Orga Lux with a bitter, reproachful smile before shrugging her shoulders.

"Orga Luxes are unlikely to betray users with whom they have a high compatibility rating, but I take it that yours has been silently assisting us? You're even more conniving than I thought, Pan-Dora," the Varda-Vaos said, seeming impressed.

"Anyway, I've been thinking about this for a while. I knew your plan was to use Erenshkigal to destroy Asterisk... But why did the Golden Bough Alliance decide to have it coincide with the final match of the Lindvolus? ...Because you needed a new symbol, that's why. So you forced Ayato to enter the tournament to keep the excitement at a fever pitch."

"That was Madiath and Dirk's idea, not mine. I would have preferred to put the plan in motion sooner without concern for the Festa. But I understood well enough that this would be the most effective course of action, so I won't complain now."

Symbol? Most effective course of action? Minato had no idea what they were talking about.

She must have let her confusion show, because Claudia broke into a soft chuckle. "This year's Lindvolus is attracting unprecedented attention. People have come from all over the world to see the Genestella competing in the tournament. That's only natural, when you consider that the second grand slam and the first Lindvolus tri-fecta in all of history are at stake. And the more excited people get, the more others who normally wouldn't be interested in the Festa will start paying attention. But yes, let's put the question of what's actually going to happen aside for a moment and consider the most likely outcome. Erenshkigal could win and secure her third consec-utive Lindvolus. The audience will shower her in adulation. Then, once the award ceremony comes around, she'll use her powers to slaughter everyone in Asterisk, and that gruesome scene will be broadcast to the world in real time... I assume you already control the broadcasters, then?"

The Varda-Vaos nodded as though that was to be expected. "Of course. The autonomous puppets can continue broadcasting even without the aid of humans."

"Now, Miss Wakamiya," Claudia asked. "What do *you* think would happen next?"

"Huh...?"

Though shaken at being addressed all of a sudden, Minato fell to thinking.

"Um... Well, Erenshkigal can't get away with it, can she? So I guess..."

"Yes. Exactly. Those cheers of adulation will give way to cries of hatred and horror... But Erenshkigal won't be alive anymore as a focus for their animosity, and they'll be looking for blood. With no one else to blame, they'll direct their fury at Genestella as a whole."

"Huh? But isn't that...a bit of a leap?"

Of course, if something like that was to happen, people *would* turn against the Genestella. But Minato couldn't believe they would resort to such violent extremes.

"If it happened anywhere else, it might be okay. But this is Asterisk, a gilded cage designed expressly to contain us Genestella. A stage for us to fight among ourselves for the enjoyment of others. Asterisk symbolizes how the lives of Genestella are controlled by ordinary people—but if it's destroyed, the sense of safety that it's supposed to guarantee will be stripped away. And that will trigger an immediate change in the attitude of the general public."

"B-but still...! It wouldn't warrant...*that*...!"

That alone shouldn't be reason enough to spark an all-out conflict.

But before she could put those thoughts into words—

"You're right," the Varda-Vaos interrupted. "It isn't enough. This is all just to create a new symbol. We will sacrifice Asterisk to create a symbol of hatred in the guise of Erenshkigal, Orphelia Landlufen. We have other efforts scheduled to be put into motion simultaneously."

"Other efforts...?"

"In response to Orphelia's show of defiance, other acts of terrorism by Genestella supremacists will soon take place all throughout the world. People will quickly discard their indifference and tolerance when their own relatives are placed in harm's way."

"You can't...!"

That *would* shift the equation.

If the seeds of hatred toward Genestella were sown not only in Asterisk but all over the world, ordinary people and Genestella would be thrown into irreconcilable conflict.

"You've brainwashed those terrorists too then, I take it?"

"You could say that. Then again, perhaps not. Most of them were already dissatisfied with the reality that Genestella are forced to endure. I merely fanned the flames a little. It *is* possible to embed feelings of hatred in a subject, but it takes considerable time and effort. That approach isn't suitable for large numbers of subjects."

"Large numbers...? How many people *have* you brainwashed?"

"I can't remember them all. Surely no less than ten thousand."

"T-ten *thousand*...?!"

Minato couldn't even imagine the destruction that would result if so many people were to engage in acts of terrorism all over the world at the same time.

"Every year, countless Genestella gather in this city from all over the world, and every year, just as many leave again for the outside. All I had to do was identify the most suitable individuals from among them. There are, of course, those who don't wish to resort to force even under my influence, but there are also those who have already established their own terrorist cells. They will gladly increase their ranks by themselves, which is naturally an immense help to us."

"But...if Genestella and ordinary people start fighting each other, wouldn't the odds of us winning be miniscule?"

Right. The groups were simply too different in number. Individual Genestella might be superior in terms of combat power, but that alone wouldn't be enough to overturn the entire global order.

"We have another plan to help with that. It is not necessary to kill all ordinary people in order for the Genestella to win. All that is required is to seize control of the true ruling class—the integrated enterprise foundations. Though at that point, the Golden Bough Alliance will no longer be involved."

The Varda-Vaos paused there for a moment, letting out a deep breath.

"...The first attempt was the Jade Twilight Incident. That failed due to my inexperience. I still didn't understand you humans, and Helga Lindwall's abilities were overwhelming. My second attempt was to bring about a new Invertia. That seemed like the most effective way to set the world in order, but that too was foiled on account of Madiath's foolish sentimentality. We were on the cusp of sending Ecknardt to the moon."

"Huh...?"

Sending him to...*the moon*?

"And now we come to the third attempt. This time, I *will* see the plan to fruition. I will permit no one to stand in my way...!"

With those words, a jet-black light gushed out from the Varda-Vaos, along with an intimidating aura underscoring the depths of her determination.

"Now that we have talked at length, perhaps you realize the futility of attempting to further interfere with our plans? If so, then leave. If you hurry, you two alone may survive."

"Oh? I doubt it," Claudia said, dismissing the Varda-Vaos's argument with a soft smile. "On the other hand, if we defeat you here, you'll lose your hold over those terrorists' minds at least, no?"

"Not necessarily. Quite a few affected by my powers will not be able to stop themselves even if released. Especially those who belong to larger organizations... Your first priority should be yourselves. Do you really think you can win?"

With those words, black light gathered around the Varda-Vaos's right hand, and a huge, distorted battle-ax took form.

Her intimidating aura was now positively murderous.

Nonetheless, Claudia maintained her cool. "Yes, of course. After all, you've always feared my friend here, haven't you?" she said, brandishing the twin blades in her hands.

"Feared? Me? Ha! What on earth are you saying…?"

"Then why take the trouble to tell us this long, meandering story of yours? It's obvious. Yes, you were trying to buy time until the end of the championship match. But most of all, you're trying to avoid fighting—against the Pan-Dora," Claudia said with a faint, knowing smile.

"…! Damn you!" the Varda-Vaos cried. A huge mass of black radiance emanated from around her as she bore down on Claudia.

"Enfield!"

Claudia, however, still fixing her foe with a sweet smile, didn't even try to avoid it.

"Huh…? What's going on…?"

"Impossible…!"

Even though Claudia had been fully engulfed by that black light that had given Minato such an intense migraine not long ago, she remained unmoving, her smile unwavering.

Instead, she gently spoke the following words: "You're an Orga Lux, and as such, a fundamentally rational being. If you could have defeated us with your powers, you wouldn't have wasted your time engaging us in conversation. The reason you didn't attempt to stop us is that you understand the true power of my friend here. Of course you do. Because both she and you are the work of Professor Ladislav Bartošik. You're practically siblings, so to speak."

Claudia's laugh was like small chimes sounding in the wind— then, the Varda-Vaos lunged toward her, ferociously slamming her battle-ax down against her defenseless foe.

And yet—

"What…?!"

"Huuuuuh?!"

The next moment, Claudia had somehow appeared *behind* the Varda-Vaos—the twin swords of the Pan-Dora aiming right for her neck with a brilliant flash.

"Tch!"

The Varda-Vaos leaped away just quickly enough to dodge the blow. For the first time, her face was awash with indignation and rage as she glowered back at her attacker.

"Oh my," Claudia remarked. "You *are* fast. I suppose a regular attack won't suffice."

"...Impossible. Impossible, impossible, impossible! You *can't* have mastered the Pan-Dora's true powers!"

Minato knew of a type of speed that operated on the level of another dimension. During her training at the Liangshan, Xinglou had moved faster than anything she had ever seen before—and while she had seemed completely invisible to the eye at first, little by little, she had gradually learned to discern her actions.

But even with her well-trained eyes, she hadn't been able to catch any of Claudia's movements just now.

Maybe she hadn't been *moving* at all. Was it possible that she had shifted instantaneously, as Sylvia had done during her quarterfinal match in the Lindvolus...?

"What was it you said before? That there is no way we could defeat you, *even using the Pan-Dora's clairvoyance*? You're probably right. Even if I exhausted my entire stock of accumulated clairvoyance, I doubt it would be enough against you. But you're too honest. You didn't say *using the Pan-Dora's powers*. Was that out of respect for your fellow Orga Lux? Or a sense of pride in her abilities? Either way..." Claudia paused there, before flashing the Varda-Vaos an altogether different kind of smile—a sneer. "You know you're doomed."

"How dare you...!" the Varda-Vaos roared, almost inarticulate.

The sound seemed not to emerge from Sylvia's throat, but from the Orga Lux itself at her chest.

Once more she lashed out with her huge jet-black ax, but a split second before the weapon could reach Claudia's neck—

Again, she somehow vanished and reappeared, this time diagonally behind her foe.

"I want you to experience for yourself the same humiliation you've inflicted on everyone you've toyed with," she said, the smile evaporating from her face. "Even if it only adds up to a millionth of their suffering,"

"Break causality—Pan-Dora."

As she uttered those words, her eyes shone with the same color as the urm-manadite of the Orga Lux she clutched in her hands.

Her eyes took on a demonic cast.

"...?!"

As those twin blades danced toward her, the Varda-Vaos swiftly raised her ax to parry them.

She should have succeeded in doing so, and yet—

"H-how...?"

The next moment, the mechanical body of the Varda-Vaos, snipped clean from Sylvia's neck, fell to the ground—while Sylvia herself, freed from the Orga Lux's powers, collapsed into a nearby flower bed.

"It's no use. You must have realized it, no? My friend's true power—the Pan-Dora's true power—is control over the laws of causality. It cannot be resisted by one such as you." With a brilliant flourish of her twin blades, precise enough to brush dewdrops from blades of grass, Claudia cast her gaze at the fallen Orga Lux.

"Causality? Control...? Not precognition...?" Minato mouthed, unable to understand what she was hearing.

Claudia fixed her with a gentle smile. "Yes. The Pan-Dora can interfere with the laws of causality. Precognition is simply a by-product of that power. If we can disrupt the relationship between cause and effect, it doesn't matter whether the Varda-Vaos uses its powers against us. The cause, her black light, would no longer lead to the effect, mental interference. Similarly, as you just saw, her attacks wouldn't lead to injury on my part, while mine would be guaranteed to hit."

"..."

Minato was left speechless, her mouth opening and closing in silence.

Wouldn't that make Claudia invincible?

"You…!"

All of a sudden, a voice reverberated in her head.

"You…! Curse you…! Primitive animals…! I won't be defeated…! I won't accept it…! Never…!"

There could be no doubt about it.

Those resentful cries belonged to none other than the Varda-Vaos itself.

Was it still trying to escape? Even ripped apart, the Orga Lux's exterior was crawling along the ground like some kind of surreal, mechanical bug.

"Goodness me… You need to learn to accept defeat," Claudia said with a sigh as she lashed out once more with her twin blades.

"Gyaaaaarrrrrgggggghhhhh!"

The Varda-Vaos, falling near Minato's feet, let out a piercing scream.

"Now, Miss Wakamiya. This is a job only you can complete."

"O-only me…?"

Come to think of it, Claudia *had* said something along those lines earlier.

"That *thing* shouldn't exist in this world. I'm not saying all Orga Luxes are like that, but this one is simply not compatible with our way of life."

Minato understood the truth of that statement, albeit only vaguely.

This Orga Lux—the Varda-Vaos—would continue to cause unrest through its very existence.

"And I'm…already at my limit," Claudia murmured, before collapsing limply to the ground.

She managed to catch herself using her twin swords as supports, but her face was lifeless, and even her faint smile seemed pained.

"A-are you all right?!"

"Oh-ho, don't worry, it isn't going to be immediate. It's just that the cost of manipulating the laws of causation is the future itself. In other words…my life span."

"…!"

This time, Minato was left well and truly speechless.

"It's okay. My life was abandoned long ago. If I can save the world in the time I have, that's good enough, don't you think?"

Still clinging to her two swords, Claudia slowly slid to rest on the floor, before catching Minato out of the corner of her eye.

"When manipulating causality, the further you diverge from what ought to have happened, the greater the price you have to pay. It wasn't such a huge amount this time."

If she was willing to go this far, then Minato too had no choice but to do whatever it took.

She had shed considerable blood, her gaze was clouding over, and she found it difficult to stand up—but even so, she mustered what power she had to lift herself to her feet.

"…I see. What do I have to do?"

"Urm-manadite isn't easy to destroy. It isn't impossible using irregular forces, as indeed Hilda Jane Rowlands did in the Lindvolus, but that would require prana on a level of someone like Erenshkigal. I suspect even Ayato and the Ser Veresta would have a challenging time of it… But you and the Járngreipr…"

So that was it.

The Járngreipr's ability was the power to freely change its own weight. That said, in actual combat, there was a limit on what was practically possible.

She preferred to adjust its mass only at the moment of impact. After all, even the slightest mistake in timing could tear her arms off at the shoulder.

But that wouldn't be an issue if her target was stationary.

Whether one ton or ten, she could increase it to whatever weight she wanted. In terms of destructive power, the Járngreipr was probably capable of standing up to any other Orga Lux.

She took a deep breath, psyched herself up, and placed her fist atop the Varda-Vaos.

But then, realizing something, she glanced across at Claudia.

"Don't worry. I've already used my precognition to check. There are only corridors beneath you, and there's no one in them all the way down to the first floor."

"Thank you!"

In that case, she could give it everything she had without needing to second-guess herself.

"*What are you…? No… Impossible?! Stop! Stop, stop, stop!*"

A panicked voice reverberated in her skull, but to Minato it was no more than white noise.

She twisted her arms and clenched her fists.

"Yaaaaarrrrrgggggghhhhh!"

"*Stopppppppppppppppppppp!*"

Her fist spun as it came crashing down, hitting the urm-manadite with its overwhelming weight.

Genkuu style—*Collapse Gouge.*

"*Aaaaaiiiiieeeeeeeeeeeeeeeeeeeeeeeeeeeeeeee!*"

The Varda-Vaos's bloodcurdling death cry echoed through her brain.

The impact easily tore through the floor, pushing the Varda-Vaos down to the building's forty-first story. But even then, there was no end to their momentum as they passed though the fortieth, the thirty-ninth, and the thirty-eighth floors—when cracks began to course through the crystalline structure of the urm-manadite.

Before she knew it, Minato's fists had penetrated through the entire building, all the way down to the entrance on the ground floor.

A shock like a violent earthquake shook the entire Hotel Elnath.

"Haah… Haah…!"

When she lifted her fists from the huge crater that had emerged beneath her, she found only the shattered remains of the urm-manadite.

"I-it's over…," she breathed heavily as she collapsed into a heap.

EPILOGUE

From his seat in the lakeside terrace café, Allekant Académie's student council president Shuuma Sakon was staring absentmindedly, his chin resting on his hands, at the face of the girl in front of him, who was busy chewing on a piece of pancake.

"...? Don't you want some, Shuuma?" Perhaps having noticed him watching her, she glanced up and offered him a fork.

"I'm fine."

"Really?"

The girl, with her fluffy curled hair, her cute glasses perched on the bridge of her nose, and her small stature and slender body, was Fevroniya Ignatovich. She might not have looked it, but she was Allekant's top-ranked fighter, the Witch of Foundational Principles, Apeiron.

In terms of overall fighting level, Allekant was said to be the weakest of Asterisk's six schools. There were multiple reasons for that, but the most obvious was the negative effect of acute factionalism. Students in practical classes were all but surrounded by various factions, and in most cases, the will of their faction took precedence over their own wishes. Similarly, it was the faction heads who decided who would participate in official ranked battles, or even whether someone *could* participate in the first place.

What's more, even performing well in the Festa was rarely enough to earn a positive appraisal, seeing as most individuals in positions of power at Allekant valued developing new technologies and weapons more than the growth or performance of the students themselves.

Given those circumstances, it was all but impossible to motivate the students in practical classes, and Allekant was famous for its students' short terms of enrollment. The most common pattern was to quickly try one's luck three times at the Festa, then graduate as soon as possible. There *were* those students who went on to the university, but they were a clear minority. And so, Allekant was regarded poorly by Festa enthusiasts and bookmakers alike. They even had a saying: *There's nothing more unreliable than the official rankings at Allekant.* Even Shuuma, the student council president himself, considered the unofficial rankings on the fansites Hexa Pantheon and Odhroerir to be much more reliable.

But even at Allekant, with its unique pecking order, the position of number one occupied a special place.

As the representative of the whole school, it symbolized their maximum strength. Neither concerns for maintaining the balance of power nor the customary bartering between factions held sway over this position. Only someone who had truly demonstrated themselves as Allekant's strongest could take on the mantle of number one.

And the face of that school, Allekant's absolute toughest Strega, was at this moment chewing on a large pancake with an utterly impassive look on her face. She might have been the school's most powerful, but no matter how you looked at her, she seemed more like a small, defenseless animal.

Why must she act up and be so selfish on today of all days...?

Yes, his position might have been merely symbolic without any real authority, but Shuuma was still the student council president. By rights, he shouldn't have been lazing around in a place like this on the day of the championship match of the Lindvolus, not with the contest about to start at any moment.

However, circumstances outside of his control had forced the matter.

Fevroniya was a treasured prodigy of the Methuselah faction, which dedicated itself to working on the basic theories of meteoric engineering and the natural laws of mana. At Allekant, students who took part in practical classes occupied a lower status than those in the research classes. Despite belonging to the former group, however, Fevroniya had earned herself a privileged status within Methuselah on account of her extremely rare abilities.

That being said, she showed exemplary dedication, seldom asserted her individuality, and quietly engaged in the research tasks assigned to her without complaint—except for once a month, when she would make some selfish demand and refuse to compromise.

For instance, she might make incomprehensible requests like *I wanna go eat some côtelette d'anillo ozomal truffle osztol frito marron chantilly!* or *I wanna go play Nine Men's Morris at an altitude of thirty thousand meters!* Sometimes, she even made trivial requests like *I wanna read my book* or *I just wanna take a nap.* In any case, if she couldn't fulfill her monthly whim, she would become extremely irritable—a prospect that Methuselah sought to avoid at all costs.

Well, Shuuma could understand why. When Fevroniya got grouchy, there was no telling what she might do. He understood that personally, to a painful extent. After all, it was his sister Chitose, the former student council president and now a popular commentator for the Festa, who had scouted Fevroniya for Allekant. Shuuma had known the girl for years.

This time, her request was a rather low-level one: *I wanna eat pancakes in a café with a view of the lake.* The problem, however, was the addendum: *With Shuuma.*

Of course, he wasn't obligated to respond to Methuselah's request. Mere figurehead or not, he *was* the student council president, and that title did come with a certain degree of official power. However, it was also true that he wanted to maintain good relations with each of the school's factions.

Shuuma may have been somewhat mediocre as a researcher and as student council president, but he took pride in his ability to negotiate with each of the varying factions and find a middle ground between their oftentimes conflicting interests.

For some time now, power dynamics at Allekant had been centered around the opposition between the Ferrovius and Pygmalion factions on the one hand and Tenorio on the other. But now, the tides were turning. Tenorio had lost its representative Hilda Jane Rowlands, and Ferrovius, the largest of all of Allekant's factions, had become disunited ever since its former head Camilla Pareto stepped down. Pygmalion may have achieved some commendable results in the Lindvolus, but it was simply too small to hold much sway over the school as a whole. And so Methuselah, which had always managed to preserve its own standing, simply couldn't be neglected.

Which was why Shuuma now found himself staring across at Fevroniya as she took another bite from her serving of pancakes.

"...You've got cream on your face, Fevroniya," he said.

"Where?"

"On your right cheek... Ah, I'll get it. Don't move."

As he reached out with a handkerchief, Fevroniya narrowed her eyes like a happy cat.

She wasn't one to show a lot of emotion, but it was clear she held a special affection for Chitose. Maybe that was why she seemed to let her guard down around Shuuma, too... It seemed logical, at least. He wasn't entirely sure.

Well, I should be able to make it in time for the award ceremony...

It was customary for the student council presidents of Asterisk's six schools to attend the award ceremony of any Festa tournament. Some, like Xinglou, tended to send proxies, but Shuuma didn't have the gall to try anything so flagrant.

With that in mind, he turned his gaze to the lake outside—when a ferry anchored at the nearby dock exploded into a sea of flames.

"Huh...?"

His jaw dropped, his eyes widening in shock.

Fortunately, the passengers had yet to board the vessel, and the crew quickly leaped into the lake to escape the conflagration.

Nonetheless, amid the shouts and screams of the milling tourists, explosion after explosion kept sounding off into the distance.

Hurrying out onto the terrace, he came across a familiar, large-bodied autonomous puppet holding a weapon and wreaking destruction.

"AR-D...? Why is *that* here...? N-no, stop! What on earth are you doing?!"

Anyone who had seen the Phoenix would know that AR-D was the property of Allekant. If the puppet rampaged through the city, the responsibility wouldn't just fall on Shuuma's shoulders—the school itself, and probably even Frauenlob, wouldn't be immune from criticism.

He rushed toward it, instructing it in a stern tone of voice to halt what it was doing, then the puppet turned his way, staring down at him in silence.

Only then did it dawn on him. The machine may have resembled AR-D, but it was something else entirely.

On top of that, looking closely, he could see that it wasn't alone. There were five in total nearby—maybe more, given the explosions erupting all over the place.

They were mass produced...? But no one ever—

...No. He wouldn't put it past her.

The individual in charge of developing the AR-D was Ernesta Kühne, the head of Pygmalion. Next to Magnum Opus, she was one of Allekant's most gifted minds—and greatest troublemakers. It wouldn't be at all surprising if she had produced more units behind the scenes.

The puppet staring down at Shuuma must have decided to treat him as a combat target, because it suddenly raised its hammer-type Lux over its head.

"Whoa...!"

Shuuma might have been a Genestella, but he belonged to the

research class, not the practical one. He had no combat training, and there was no way that he would be able to fight a puppet on the level of AR-D.

The hammer swung down with tremendous speed, only to be easily blocked as a new figure swept in front of him.

"Fevroniya…!"

Having caught the blow in her right hand, she was holding open a thick book in her left.

"…What are you doing?"

It wasn't clear whether she was addressing Shuuma with that comment or the autonomous puppet. Nonetheless, it was obvious from her tone of voice that she was in a particularly bad mood. After all, her wish—*"I wanna eat pancakes with Shuuma in a café with a view of the lake"*—had been unceremoniously interrupted.

Fevroniya squeezed the hammer-type Lux with her right hand, then lightly tapped the puppet on the chest as though knocking on a door.

The next moment, its entire body vanished without a trace.

Did she just rewrite Newton's laws of motion…?

Fevroniya's ability—*Apeiron's* ability—was control over the laws of physics.

Newton's second law of motion simply stated that mass and acceleration determined the magnitude of any given force, but Fevroniya had adjusted it so that even small amounts of mass and acceleration could result in a tremendous quantity of force.

And that wasn't all.

It looked like she had also altered the third law—that for every action, there is always an equal reaction. Otherwise, her small hand would have been crushed to a pulp just now.

"Do you mind not interrupting?" she murmured.

Fevroniya always spoke in a questioning tone, irrespective of the occasion or who she was addressing—as if to suggest there were still so many things she didn't understand about the world.

Soon, the remaining puppets gathered around them.

And without even the slightest change to her expression, Fevroniya turned the page of the book in her left hand.

It was blank—or rather, the entire book was blank. It seemed she used the pages for her calculations to compose new laws of physics. She didn't need to use a pen, though—her eyes alone were enough to inscribe the changes. In other words, this blank book was her weapon and the medium for her abilities.

She raised her right hand into the air and clenched her fist.

At that moment, the puppets let out a crackling sound and crumbled together like a ball of wastepaper. Before long, they had been reduced to the size of a pebble, floating in the air at first, then falling heavily to the ground. Given the way the object dug into the pavement with a hard thud, the mass must have remained the same. Shuuma couldn't even begin to guess what laws of physics had been adjusted this time.

"Let's go back, Shuuma?" Fevroniya said, tilting her head to one side and glancing at him as though nothing at all was out of the ordinary.

By *go back*, no doubt she meant the terrace café, not Allekant.

But this was no time for that. Explosions and fires continued to burst up all across the city. He had to figure out what on earth was going on, and naturally, he had plenty of questions for Ernesta.

Yet…right now, he couldn't refuse her request.

"Ah… All right. I'll tag along," he said with a heavy sigh before following after her.

Everything would have wait until Fevroniya's whim had been fulfilled.

There were no other customers or even staff left in the café—no doubt they had all fled. Returning to their table amid the scattered and upturned chairs, Fevroniya set to consuming what remained of her half-eaten pancakes.

"…If you would have at least entered the Festa, it would make my job as student council president a little easier," Shuuma grumbled in resignation.

Fevroniya nibbled at her meal, washed it down, then said, "You know I hate fighting, right?"

"Yes, yes, I know," Shuuma said, his shoulders drooping.

That was why she so rarely participated in official ranked battles. Besides, Methuselah wasn't willing to let her enter the Festa anyway. They would sooner use her powers to advance their research than let her waste her time on something as trivial as fighting.

Still, he couldn't help but wonder…

If she *had* signed up for the tournament, maybe it would have been her in the championship arena today.

*

The elevator doors opened onto a vast, sprawling space.

It was a hexagonal field, perhaps modeled on the Festa stage. A pillar stood at every corner, each of which housed an elevator.

No sooner had Ayato and Saya stepped out onto the field—the site of the illegal Eclipse tournament—than a voice called out to them from the darkness.

"Well, well, well. So we have a pair of uninvited guests."

Far across the field, perched atop the wreckage of a collapsed pillar, sat a man, fixing them both with a faint smile. The figure, his face behind a mask, garbed in the white battle jacket used by Eclipse fighters, spread his arms wide as he rose to his feet.

"But now that you're here, welcome, Ayato Amagiri, Saya Sasamiya! I was just thinking how it would feel a little lonely to watch this city's demise all by myself."

"…Madiath Mesa," Ayato murmured through clenched teeth.

The head of the Festa Executive Committee and one-time champion of the Phoenix.

A regular fighter at the Eclipse under the guise of his alias Lamina Mortis, and the user of the Orga Lux the Raksha-Nada.

The one who had tormented Ayato's older sister Haruka, his own biological daughter.

And, right now, he was also the leader of the Golden Bough Alliance, intent on destroying Asterisk and as a result, inflicting unimaginable pain on Ayato's dear partner Julis.

"...We're here to stop you," Ayato said, activating the Ser Veresta.

"Hmm... A little impatient, aren't we? How about we enjoy the entertainment first? I'm sure you want to see how your little scheme plays out, no?"

With a snap of his fingers, Madiath summoned up enough air-windows to fill the field, more than Ayato could possibly count.

And displayed on those screens—

"Kirin...! And Sylvia and Claudia...!"

In the air-window Saya pointed to, Kirin could be seen engaging in combat with Percival, while Claudia was likewise in the midst of battle against the Varda-Vaos.

Not only that, others showed Stjarnagarm officers confronting huge swathes of Valiants, busy destroying facilities all throughout the city.

"These are all real-time images from our Valiant units. Oh, there's no need to worry. The puppets' job is just to destroy any escape routes and distract the city guard."

In any event, it looked like Claudia's group had successfully reached the Varda-Vaos.

Thank goodness... At least the first step was a success.

All that remained was to trust them to finish the job.

"...Oh? Is that Minato Wakamiya alongside Miss Enfield?" Madiath said as he watched the video, surprise evident in his voice.

"Minato...?"

When had they found time to call her?

But there could be no mistaking it—that was Minato fighting by Claudia's side.

"Well, I suppose she has the right. As far as I'm concerned, she can do as she wishes."

"The *right*...? So it's true! You *were* behind the accident that killed her father!" Ayato cried furiously.

Minato had lost her father when an experimental rocket engine that he was working on had supposedly malfunctioned and exploded. Ayato had long suspected that the Golden Bough Alliance was involved, but to hear Madiath practically admit to it...

"Yes, we needed the rocket engine. Desperately," Madiath said with a shake of his head. "It was Varda's sole decision to stage the accident... But I do believe her actions were regrettable."

"How dare you...?!"

Madiath's words had been totally devoid of emotion.

Fresh anger welled up in the pit of Ayato's stomach. To have such utter disregard for human life...

"I never expected you to get this far at this point in the game. It's reckless, this plan of yours, but it's considered, too. It's true we can't contact Miss Orphelia right now... But let's just see how long *she* can keep that up."

Madiath turned his gaze to another air-window, one that showed Julis in the heat of battle against Orphelia.

It was a live feed of the championship match.

The two contestants were throwing everything they had against each other, letting loose with their abilities.

"Julis will be fine. All we have to do is finish here before she finishes there."

"Ayato's right. We won't let you get away with this," Saya added, activating her Helnekraum and pointing the muzzle straight at Madiath.

"I see. So you've both come for me, while Miss Enfield and her companions are going for Varda. But you do realize we have a third comrade? Unfortunately, we don't have any Valiants with him, so I don't have any footage, but I wonder how things are going on his end?"

"That's..."

Right.

There were three ringleaders behind the Golden Bough Alliance— Madiath Mesa, the Varda-Vaos, and Dirk Eberwein. Even if Ayato and Saya managed to defeat Madiath and Claudia's team was able to take out the Varda-Vaos, so long as Dirk remained, there could be no stopping Orphelia.

Eishirou was supposed to be on the Tyrant's trail, and yet…

"Ha-ha, you're a bad liar. The truth is written right there on your face." Madiath chuckled as he looked Ayato over. "This is good timing. Let's call him and see how he's doing."

With those words, he pulled his mobile from his pocket and opened a new air-window.

"*…Tch! We were just getting to the interesting part! What now? This had better be important.*" The surly red-haired youth on the other end of the line clicked his tongue in annoyance.

"Oh, it's certainly important," Madiath answered with a theatrical wave of his hand. "Varda and I have been visited by *unexpected guests*. I was worried about you, my friend."

"*Ah, I get it. Sounds like you've got a bit of mess on your hands. But don't worry. Nothing out of the ordinary over here.*"

"Excellent. So everything is proceeding according to plan?"

"*It will,*" Dirk answered blithely, before shifting his hate-filled gaze. "*Yo, Ayato Amagiri. Your buddy Yabuki was sniffing around… Sorry, but he ain't found me.*"

"Ngh…!"

Ayato couldn't tell whether Claudia's plan had somehow been leaked or whether Dirk had hidden himself exceptionally well, but if Eishirou couldn't find him, it would have been hopeless even if Ayato and the others had helped.

"I wouldn't be so sure," Saya said. "I don't trust Yabuki as a person, but I have confidence in his skills. He'll find you before time runs out."

"*Ha! You don't even have your head on straight, do you?*" Dirk shot back condescendingly. "*Where exactly do you think I am? An airship. Up in the sky. No matter what you do, it's impossible for you lot to get to me here.*"

Up in the sky…?!

That *would* make it difficult for Eishirou to track him down.

It might be *possible*, but in the limited time they had left…

"Wonderful. You seem to be doing remarkably well. I'm envious," Madiath interrupted, applauding theatrically. "By the way, I do have one question."

"Huh? And what's that?"

"Why did you betray us when we're so close to fulfilling our goals?"

"…!"

In contrast to Madiath's perilous words, his tone of voice was light, his smile unwavering.

"Hmph. So you caught on?" For his part, Dirk didn't seem fazed in the least, admitting to the accusation without hesitation.

"Of course. All our information told us their group had no idea of our true purpose or whereabouts. For them to have acted so aggressively over the past twelve hours, it's only natural to suspect a leak. Wouldn't you agree?"

"Just so you know, I didn't give them squat about Orphelia. She probably gave that up herself. All I did was offer them a couple of hints about where to find you and Varda," Dirk said unapologetically.

"…What does that mean?" Saya said, staring at Madiath and Dirk, eyebrows raised in suspicion.

It was only thanks to the information that Dirk had provided Eishirou that Ayato and the others had been able to locate Madiath and the Varda-Vaos, and even after confirming its accuracy, he hadn't been able to shake the suspicion that it was all a trap. But it seemed like the members of the Golden Bough Alliance really were turning against themselves.

"I thought all three of us were in consensus when it came to the implementation of the plan, even if we each had different agendas. For you to try to upend it all at this critical juncture… I find it difficult to comprehend," Madiath said, sighing deeply as his shoulders slumped.

"Difficult to comprehend? Yeah, I guess it is. If you had ever

bothered to understand even the first thing about me, you would've known I'd do this. Come on, as far as you're concerned, Varda and I are no different from the rest of them, are we? To you, we're all equally worthless." Dirk's voice lowered even further, his frustration emanating through the air-window.

And it wasn't just frustration. Ayato could clearly *feel* the black depths of his hatred, his disgust, his resentment, his anger, and a swathe of other negative emotions swirling around him.

"Listen up, Madiath Mesa. Yeah, I hate this screwed up world. So I teamed up with you and Varda to destroy it. To force all the winners, those worthless integrated enterprise foundations included, to crawl down in the filth with the rest of us."

To destroy the world.

So that was the goal of this young man, the famed Tyrant. Ayato was immediately convinced of the veracity of his words.

This, he felt, was the true Dirk Eberwein.

"But I hate you just as much as these guys do. You cling to the past, wallowing in your pathetic delusions and your pointless anger. I don't much like Varda either, what with how she's always looking down her nose on our world, chasing after her stupid fantasies. Or Orphelia, running away from her own damn responsibility. Or Percival, letting her natural talents rot. Or you, Ayato Amagiri. You're an eyesore and a goddamn pain in the ass."

Dirk's outburst wasn't emotional, but neither was he speaking calmly or matter-of-factly—rather, this tirade was delivered deliberately, with a deep, dark passion.

"If I had kept silent, nothing would have stopped us from winning. A complete and total victory... But I can't just sit by and let someone I hate win. And that goes for everyone, myself included. I hate myself just as much as the rest of you. I make myself sick. So I thought I'd stir things up a little. But don't feel bad. If things keep going like they are, the plan will still work out, even if it's not exactly how you intended. You might not get everything you wanted, but neither will they. Both sides will lose. Yeah, you heard me. We'll all lose. You, me, Varda,

Ayato Amagiri, the integrated enterprise foundations, everyone in this whole shitty world. We'll all wind up in a nasty, miserable place, stuck dragging each other down, none of us ever winning."

Then, in the softest of murmurs, Dirk finished, "And that'll make me feel just a little better about it all."

AFTERWORD

Hi there. Yuu Miyazaki here.

I'm really, really sorry for the long wait leading up to this volume. There were a bunch of reasons for the delay, but it was ultimately my responsibility, so I'd like to offer my sincerest apologies.

Now, as usual, this afterword contains spoilers, so please be warned if you haven't yet finished reading.

In the main story, the Golden Bough Alliance's plan has finally been revealed, and the decisive battle against them has gotten underway. For that reason, I'd like to start there. First of all, we have the battle against Percival. In short, she's just like Orphelia in a way. Percival's sense of self-identity comes from her tremendous loss, while Orphelia manages to maintain her mental balance by surrendering everything—lock, stock, and barrel. From Dirk's perspective, people like these two, who lean wholly on *one major element*, so to speak, are basically just pawns that can be easily entrapped. Kirin was once pretty similar—dedicated entirely to honing her swordsmanship— but since then she has managed to grow as a human being. If you consider this, I think it will give deeper meaning to their fight.

And then there's the battle against Varda. The time has finally come for her—well, let's say *her* for now—as the keystone of the

Golden Bough Alliance and the root of all evil, to finally meet her fate. The way it played out wasn't out of respect for the Gray Witch precisely, but a character who takes over other people's bodies couldn't meet their end any other way. Claudia hadn't had an active scene for a while, so I decided to show her off using the most powerful cheat ability in all of Asterisk's history. Drawing on the true power of the Pan-Dora, no doubt she would be able to snatch victory even on the stage of the Festa itself (although, of course, she would have to pay a considerable price in doing so). As for Varda's end, I decided to leave that to Minato back when I started writing the side story volumes. The only question was whether to have her intentionally avenge her father's death or have her do so unknowingly. In the end, I decided on the latter option, which felt more in keeping with her character.

As for the remaining three members of the Golden Bough Alliance—Dirk, Madiath, and Orphelia—I'll leave that for the next volume, which will be the conclusion of the whole story. I hope you'll keep reading until the very end.

Last but not least, I'd like to thank everyone who helped bring this volume to completion.

To okiura for the wonderful cover illustration, to my editor O, to the editorial staff and my proofreaders, and most of all, to you, my readers, for your continued support—thank you. I look forward to seeing you all again in the next volume.

Yuu Miyazaki,
October 2021